WOLF'S MIDLIFE BITE

MARKED OVER FORTY

MEG RIPLEY

SHIFTER NATION

Disclaimer

This book is intended for readers age 18 and over. It contains
mature situations and language that may be objectionable to some
readers.

CONTENTS

WOLF'S MIDLIFE BITE

WOLF'S MIDLIFE BITE

MARKED OVER FORTY

1

"BRODY, I COULD REALLY USE YOUR HELP!"

Immediately, Brody dropped his pencil and shot to his feet. Adrenaline coursed through his veins, and his wolf was ready. "What's up?"

Poppy smiled at him from the doorway of his booth. "I pulled you out of a sketch again, didn't I?"

"Shit." The last time Poppy had asked for help, the frat boy she'd been tattooing thought being alone in her booth meant he could get more than just artwork. She had plenty of bite and knew how to put just about any customer in their place, but her small stature tended to make men think they could take things further. That didn't seem to be the case right now. "You're good?"

"With that," she said, knowing what he meant.

"I'm just running behind. My next appointment just got here, but the shading on this sleeve is taking way longer than I thought it would."

"Squirmer?" Brody had caught a glimpse of the muscled man when he'd come in a couple of hours ago, his head thrown back and his shoulders wide.

"Yup," she confirmed quietly. "He's asked me to take so many breaks, I'll be lucky if I finish by the end of the week."

That figured. It happened all the time in their shop, and Poppy tended to overbook herself. "What's your next one getting?"

"Just a small coverup." Poppy handed him her original drawing and the stencil, which she already had ready to go. "Can I send her in?"

It wasn't anything particularly exciting, just a bird flying out of a cage, but he was more than capable. Brody took a wistful glance at the pencil drawing he'd been lost in before Poppy had asked for his help. He'd made a smudge when he'd dropped his pencil, but he could fix that later. The tattoos were what paid the bills, anyway. "Sure."

He prepped his booth while Poppy explained the situation to her customer. Brody was filling a cap with black ink when he heard the shuffle of footsteps and looked up.

She made his breath catch in his throat. Her strawberry blonde hair fell in delicate waves to her jawline, and her bright green eyes easily picked up the intense light of the booth. She hung back a little, hugging an arm around her waist.

"Come on in," he said, hoping he sounded casual even though he definitely didn't feel that way inside. Brody saw all sorts of people in this line of work, and at this point, they were all just canvases for his artwork. But this one was making his wolf churn inside him. He realized he'd overfilled the ink cap and cursed quietly to himself.

"Um, I don't know," she hedged, taking only one step further toward the chair. "Maybe I should reschedule with Poppy for another time."

"You'd probably have to wait a while before you could get back in with her," Brody replied. "She's usually booked out for a couple of months."

His potential customer bit her lip and nodded. "Yeah, I guess I already knew that. Why aren't *you*?"

Brody found himself smiling at the sassy question. It caught him off-guard, but he liked it. "I am, actually, but I purposely schedule some free time to catch up on my artwork."

"Oh." Her eyes lifted to the paintings and sketches lining the walls of the booth. "I see."

He was used to people checking out his work. It was his job, after all, and the more confidence people had in his skill, the more likely they were to come to him. It also meant they paid more. Now, though, he felt oddly exposed. He tipped his head toward the chair. "You can stay or reschedule with Poppy. It's up to you."

"Um. I guess so." She moved slowly as though she were trying to force her feet forward. "I'm sorry for being so weird. It's just that I was planning on having a female artist. No offense to you, it's just..." She gestured toward her body.

Brody's eyes landed on the spot she referred to, just inside her hipbone. People got tattoos all over their bodies, and it was his job to figure out how the planes of that canvas suited the artwork. It was all routine, yet he felt his heart jump into his throat.

"I've seen *everything* over the last few decades as a tattoo artist. Trust me, you have nothing to worry about," he assured her as he closed the booth's door for her privacy. "Why don't you have a seat. I see you've got leggings on. Good choice. You can just roll down the top and show me what we're covering up." He washed up, snapped on a pair of gloves, and grabbed a paper towel.

"Okay." Her breath became ragged as she tried to

do as he asked. She wiggled in the chair as she fought with the waistband of her leggings, trying to show him her tattoo without exposing anything else.

Brody tried not to look, knowing that would only make things worse, but it was clear she wasn't making any progress. "Can I help?" he asked.

She let out a frustrated sigh. "Don't bother. It's just not going to happen. I'm sorry."

"Come on, don't be so hard on yourself." With expert hands, he pulled down one side of her leggings to expose the "Property of JC" tattoo just inside her right hipbone. To keep the stretchy fabric in place, he tugged it down on the left side as well so it wouldn't just roll back up. Tucking the paper towel around the roll he'd created, he nodded at his own work. "There."

"Um, isn't that a little far?" Her face flushed as red as her hair as she reached down to cover herself.

He hadn't meant to embarrass her, but he had a job to do. "I have to be able to get to the tattoo to cover it, you know."

"Right."

He rubbed down the area with an alcohol prep pad. "What's your name?" It was usually a question he asked *before* he pulled a woman's pants down, but whatever. Maybe small talk would help.

"Robin. Wait, what are you doing now?"

He stopped with the disposable razor in the air over her skin. "Shaving you."

"Oh, god. I'm not that hairy down there, am I?"

Brody chuckled as he went about his work. "No. I have to do this, no matter how fine the hair is. You won't get a good clean tat, otherwise." He held her soft skin taught as he ran the razor over it.

The smell of peaches mixed with the warm, velvety scent of her skin. She was human, he could tell, but her scent was entirely different from the others. Something about her was driving his wolf crazy. Brody focused on his goal, eyeing the fuzzy, crooked letters inked into her skin as he ran an alcohol wipe over them once again. "Where did you have this done?"

An angry huff emanated from her throat. "You don't want to know."

"I probably already do," he murmured as he picked up the stencil. "I guess that means you're not going to tell me who JC is, either."

She pressed her lips together.

He rolled a shoulder as he carefully placed the stencil. "You don't have to, but people usually have some pretty big life events attached to their tattoos. Coverups are like therapy."

Robin was silent for a moment, and Brody could tell just by having the side of his hand against her that every muscle in her body was tense. "JC is my ex," she finally admitted.

"Mm." Not a surprise. He wouldn't have ever done a tattoo like that for someone. The only names he was comfortable with permanently inking onto clients were those of kids, pets, or loved ones who'd passed on. It was pretty safe that those relationships wouldn't change, unlike this one.

"He was the one who did it, too," she volunteered.

"I kind of figured that." The faded, blown-out lines were the first clue, along with the inconsistently-sized letters. Brody grabbed a hand mirror and showed her the stencil. "How's that?"

It was obvious that she'd been trying to avoid looking at him or what he was doing, but she gave a blink of surprise as she looked at the reflection. "Is that really going to cover the whole thing?

"Like it was never there," he replied confidently. Coverups could be a bitch, but Poppy had done a good job of designing this one so that the cage's base covered JC's masterpiece completely.

"Then yeah." A hint of a smile played on her lips.

"Cool. I'm going to lay you down to make this a

little easier." He pushed the foot pedal that reclined the chair all the way back. It jolted to life, making her curves jiggle a little. Brody really needed to keep his focus on the work. "So, was this your idea?"

Robin snorted a little as she adjusted herself on the chair. She had her arms pulled up over her chest to keep them out of the way, but at least they were relaxed now. "No, not exactly. JC was super controlling, and he liked the idea. He kept bugging the hell out of me to do it, especially once he'd ordered a kit so that he could start practicing to be an artist. I was young and dumb, and he managed to convince me one night after I'd been drinking. The evidence of what happened is all right there."

Picking up his machine, Brody tested the mechanism before dipping the needle in black ink. He'd seen all sorts of bad tats, but this one pissed him off. It was total crap, for one thing, and no one should be tattooing at home, especially on someone under the influence. But it wasn't just the ethics, cleanliness, or even the lack of artistry. Some asshole had put his stamp on this woman. He adjusted his grip, forcing himself to loosen up a little, but his wolf wasn't having it. The beast lashed out inside him, snarling at the idea of her being anyone's property but his own.

"So, is this JC an artist somewhere now?" Brody asked, almost hoping he was so he could go find him when he was done.

"Nope," she said with a snicker. "That was just one of the many great things he thought he was going to do. He did this one, and then he did what was supposed to be a dog on his friend's back. It looked more like Cousin Itt from *The Addams Family*, and he gave up."

The buzzing of the machine echoed through the room as Brody ran a long, clean line around the outside of the cage. "Sounds like a fucking winner."

"Well, you know what they say. There's a reason he's an ex."

And it was a damn good thing he was. The lines at the corners of Brody's eyes deepened as he tried to focus on his work, but he could just imagine what he'd do to this prick if he were still around. His wolf liked the idea of tearing him apart, piece by piece. He started on the inner lines of the cage, not even needing to ask Robin what this symbolized. She was free now.

He liked to lose himself in his artistry, but it wouldn't happen today. Not while he was so close to her. Even bent over her like this, with his hands touching her, his face so close to her delicate skin, it wasn't enough. Her scent was utterly intoxicating, tempting his wolf to make an appearance. He needed a distraction. "So, where do you work?"

"Oh. I'm a dental hygienist."

"Yeah? How long have you been doing that?" Brody swapped to his other machine with a shading needle, filling in the base of the birdcage and covering JC's work. It filled him with deep satisfaction to make those words disappear.

"Oh, just about twenty years now." She was finally starting to relax, her muscles loosening the longer she lay there. "I went to hygiene school right after high school, and I've been cleaning teeth ever since."

Next came the bird itself, and he switched to a bright blue ink. "You know, I've got a tooth that's been bothering me. You came to see me at my office, so maybe I should come see you at yours."

"Well, we're usually booked about two months in advance."

Brody looked up and saw the sarcastic smile on her face. "So I hear. I guess I'll have to make an appointment right away, then."

"You should," she smiled. "How's it looking?"

"You're done." Brody wiped down her skin, knowing this wouldn't be the last time he'd touch it.

"Are you serious? I hardly even felt a thing!" She pushed herself up onto her elbows.

Scooting back on his stool, Brody hit the foot pedal to raise her back to a seated position. "That's what happens when you come to a professional. Go check it out." He pointed toward the full-length mirror in the back corner of his booth.

Robin's modesty seemed to fly out the window as she raced over to the mirror with her waistband still rolled down, holding her tummy up to study her new work. She was too focused on what Brody had done for her. "This is incredible. I can't thank you enough."

"It's not a problem. I've got some aftercare sheets for you, and you can always call if you have any questions." Brody stripped off his gloves and pulled the papers out of a nearby file, the standard for every customer. But that only gave him another minute with her before he sent her out to pay at the front.

"Thanks." Adjusting her pants, she reached for her purse. "And here's the card for my office, if you really do want to have that tooth evaluated."

His fingers brushed hers as he took it, energy crackling between them and straight up his arm. "I'll see you there."

2

_____

"EAT UP, BUT SAVE SOME ROOM. I'VE GOT HOMEMADE cheesecake for dessert!" Elaine Cassidy eagerly rolled her hands through the air to encourage her two daughters to get their forks back into their mouths as quickly as possible.

"Mom." Robin looked at the tender roast beef, buttery mashed potatoes, and creamed corn on her plate. "I can't keep eating like this every time I come here."

"Don't tell me you're trying to watch your weight." Her mother gestured with a serving spoon as she gave Robin a firm look. Elaine wasn't a particularly small woman herself, but she'd always taught her girls that there was much more to life than being a size zero.

"I'm not," Robin replied. "I could care less about the calories. It's the saturated fat. I'm forty years old, and I have to think about these things if I want to live another forty years."

"It's a nice, balanced meal," her father replied as he generously spooned gravy over his plate. "And potatoes are good for you."

"Not when they're drenched in butter," Robin retorted. Her last physical had gone well, but her cholesterol was slowly creeping upward, sparking a lecture about how these things start happening with age. She shook her head, hoping she wouldn't have to revisit that topic next year.

"Don't bother," Renee advised as she stabbed a few small strips of meat and put them on her daughter's plate. "They don't listen. I told them that two years ago, but they're still living in the fifties."

"Oh, you girls are terrible!" their mother scolded, but they all laughed.

A deep sense of happiness bloomed in Robin's chest. Family dinners had been a tradition for as long as she could remember. Her parents had toted her and Renee to their grandparents' house every Sunday. Though her grandma and grandpa were gone now, the custom carried on with only a change in venue. It was comforting to know that no matter what was happening in her life, she could always count on this.

"I don't *want* gravy," Kennedy protested, scowling at the dripping spoon that Renee had just lifted out of the gravy boat. She held her hands protectively over her roast beef. "It looks gross."

"I know it doesn't look that pretty, but it tastes good. You should try it, at least."

Kennedy, sharp and observant even at just eight years old, glanced around the table. "Aunt Robin doesn't have any on her plate."

Renee gave her a pleading look.

She didn't even need to ask. Robin held out her plate. "I'd love some, please." So much for making this meal even the least bit healthy.

"Fine." Kennedy reluctantly moved her hands so her mother could drizzle a bit of gravy over one end of the meat.

"Oh, shoot. I almost forgot. Kennedy's class is doing their concert on Tuesday night if any of you can make it." Renee beamed proudly at her daughter, who was ignoring the adult talk and sneering at her gravy.

Robin sighed. "Sorry, Tuesdays are when Dr. Watson does his special late nights for patients who can't come in during the workday. He wouldn't dare let me off unless I gave him a month's notice or a signed doctor's note."

Kennedy sat up a little straighter. "That's okay. We suck anyway."

"I'm sure you don't," Renee corrected gently.

Her daughter let out a bark of sarcastic laughter that sounded far more mature than her eight years should allow. "You haven't been there during practice. We're supposed to clap along to the first song. You know, to the beat. But Gabriel is off every time, no matter how much Mrs. Collins goes over it."

"I don't think that's the end of the world, kiddo," Ed Cassidy noted with a smile.

"Grandpa, Lucy screeches instead of singing," Kennedy went on, undeterred. "It's like she's trying really hard to sound like an opera singer, but it's horrible. Mrs. Collins put her all the way in the back where she won't be as close to the microphones, but I don't think it's going to make much of a difference. She's so loud."

"Sounds like I won't be missing much," Robin said with a barely suppressed laugh. She would've gladly put up with Lucy's screeching and Gabriel's off-time clapping if it meant she got to see Kennedy perform, but it was getting harder and harder to do these days.

"You know, Robin, I heard Dr. Sweeney across town has an opening for a hygienist," Mrs. Cassidy commented as she shook a thick layer of pepper over her meat.

She pressed her hand to her heart and rolled her head back. "I wish."

"Well, then why don't you just put your application in?" her father suggested as he grabbed the bowl of mashed potatoes and added a heaping second helping to his plate. "The worst they can do is say no."

"Actually, the worst they can do is say yes and then tell me just how little they're going to pay me," Robin corrected. "I'd love to work for a pediatric dentist, but I can't give up the paycheck I'm getting at Dr. Watson's right now. Not after all the attorney's fees with the divorce and running a house on one income."

"You could always move back in here," Mrs. Cassidy suggested. "Your room is right where you left it, Nirvana posters and all."

"Oh my god, Mom. No." Robin knew she was lucky to have parents who supported her in anything and everything she did. They'd even tolerated her when she was in sixth grade and thought she was destined to be a drummer in the next big grunge band. That alone should've made them saints, but there was no way in hell she could move back in with her parents at this point.

Her mother rolled one shoulder. "It's just an idea. You've been complaining about working for Dr. Watson for quite some time now."

"That man must've made a deal with the devil to run such a successful business," her father commented. "I never knew of a dentist's office that kept the sorts of hours he does. Even with that, you can't get an appointment for anything."

Robin poked her fork at her vegetables. She really loved being able to help people, and she was particularly good at comforting them when they came in terrified of the place. She hadn't been able to do that part of her job lately. There was no time for friendly chitchat with her patients. As soon as she was finished, she had to shove them out the door and prepare for the next one. Her job had turned into a paycheck instead of a career. Right now, though, she needed that paycheck. "Yeah, and he can be a total jerk sometimes. The thing is, with the expensive procedures and sheer volume of work he does, he can afford to pay a lot more than anyone else around Eugene. That's quite the carrot dangling in front of me every morning when I look at myself in the mirror and decide if I'm going to work."

Kennedy turned to Renee. "Can I do that, Mom?"

"What?"

"Look at myself in the mirror in the morning and decide if I'm going to school," Kennedy explained.

Renee's lips tightened into a hard line, and she was silent for a moment. "No, honey. You have to go to school. You already know this."

Leaning back and rubbing his full stomach, Ed asked, "Did you see that thing on the news about that young woman that's gone missing?"

His wife elbowed him in the ribs and nodded toward Kennedy. "I don't think that's exactly dinner table talk."

"I'm full. Can I go outside to play?" Kennedy had already pushed her chair back from the table, barely waiting for the answer and clearly not worried about anything her grandfather had to say.

"I'll come with you," Robin volunteered. Spending time with her niece was an easy excuse to get out of the cheesecake that would inevitably be offered momentarily.

"I think I could use a little fresh air, myself." Renee grabbed her plate and Kennedy's and brought them to the sink.

A few minutes later, Robin and Renee stood under the massive oak tree in the backyard. It was the same tree they used to turn into a fort by throwing a blanket over one of the lowest branches, the same tree whose wide trunk had hidden them when they'd first tried a little pot. Now it was the tree that sheltered them from the evening sun as they watched Kennedy run around with their parents' old Labrador, Sunny.

"I swear he loses about half of the years on him when she comes over to play," Renee commented as she folded her arms in front of her chest and smiled. "He's straight from couch potato to Olympic champion as soon as she shows up."

Robin had to agree. A tattered rope toy dangled from Kennedy's hand as the dog zoomed after her. The girl was squealing with delight, and Robin was sure Sunny would be, too, if he could. "You're so lucky to have her. She's the closest I'll ever come to having a kid of my own."

"Hey, you never know. I mean, now that JC is out of the picture." Renee waggled her eyebrows suggestively.

"Right, because high cholesterol and reading glasses are the perfect prerequisites for pregnancy." Robin shook her head, knowing so much time had been wasted. There was no point in dwelling on it, though. She still had a whole life to live ahead of her. She just had to figure out what that meant.

"Speaking of JC, did you go through with getting that nasty old tattoo covered up? I felt bad that I couldn't go with you, but with Ben out of town for work, I'm on full-time mom duty." She glanced over at her charge, who was now engaged in a game of tug-of-war with Sunny.

"That's okay. I can't say it all went as planned, but I did it." Turning her back toward the house, Robin pulled down her leggings and held up her muffin top. "I think it turned out pretty good, though."

Renee let out a long, low whistle. "That's a hell of a lot better than JC's piece. But what happened? I thought you really liked Poppy when you went in for your consultation."

Poppy had come highly recommended by Renee, some of her tattooed friends, and patients. Though Robin hadn't looked forward to reliving that painful experience, she'd felt better about going through it with a female artist. "I did, but she was overbooked when I got there. She apologized a million times, then set me up with this other artist in the shop. I wasn't thrilled about showing him my FUPA, but he was a real professional."

"And?" Renee pressed. "I bet he was hot."

Readjusting her clothes, Robin felt one corner of her mouth twitch upwards. "Yeah, which made it that much harder! I was mortified and almost canceled completely. I wasn't even sure I could deal with having the top of my pants down, but then he did it for me."

"Well, damn. I think you might be getting more action than I am. Kennedy, make sure you don't pull too hard!" She watched her daughter for another moment before she turned her attention back to Robin.

She was laughing. "I wouldn't call it that. He just knew what needed to happen to get the job done, and he was doing Poppy a favor by taking over. I think he wanted to get back to his drawing." It wasn't like he'd been cold and distant, though. He was probably just trying to get through the appointment and get her out the door. But Brody had been sweet, getting her to talk so she would relax. Once the conversation had gotten rolling, Robin had been so comfortable with him that she was shocked when it was all over.

"So, are you going to go back for another tattoo?" Renee asked in a teasing, singsong voice. "Are you going to ask him out?"

Robin laughed again. "No, thanks. He's hot and very talented, but it ends there." There had been that definitive spark between them when she'd handed him her business card. Robin had thought about it a lot, with that jolting feeling surging through her veins every time as though it were happening all over again.

"Come on." Renee bumped her with her hip. "You could use something to shake your life up a little."

"I've had it shaken up enough for now, thank you very much. I'm a newly minted single woman now that JC is out of the picture, and I'm more than happy to let things settle down for a while." Brody was exciting and different. He wasn't arrogant like JC, and that contrast was appealing. The logical part of her knew she'd be equally attracted to anyone else who didn't remind her of her ex. For now, she had everything she needed in her life.

"Aunt Robin!" Kennedy puffed as she came running up. "Do you want to play tag with me?"

Robin smiled. She hadn't played tag since she was a kid. She didn't have the same kind of stamina that she did back then, and she sure wasn't as fast. But that was all right. Kennedy could tag her every time, and she'd be thrilled. "You're on, kid!"

3

BRODY DREW A LONG, CURVING LINE AND THEN another that reflected the general shape. He sneered at the result, though he knew a drawing could sometimes be saved if he pursued it a little. His eccentric junior high art teacher, Mrs. Monroe, had taught him that. "So what if it's not what you thought it was going to be?" she'd ask, throwing her hands in the air and making the brilliantly colored fabric of her caftan swirl. "Change it, make it something different! Maybe it was never meant to be your original idea, anyway."

That'd been hard to wrap his head around, but it'd worked well both in his personal pursuit of art as well as his professional one. It made him adapt to his canvas, to his subject, and even to his mood.

Right now, though, that particular ideal wasn't helping him. He flicked to the next page in his sketchbook and tried again. Robin had been beautiful. He wanted to capture the curve of her cheek, the softness of her hair, and the graceful way she tipped her head when she was uncertain. The light in her eyes and the flush of her full, pink lips would have to come later, when he'd moved past the basic sketch. Oil pastels. Yeah. That would be perfect for her.

That spark, though, that shot of electricity that had clenched his gut and aroused his wolf, that would be impossible to capture.

"What do you think, Brody?"

"Hm?"

Rex sighed as he tapped the hard back of Brody's sketchbook. "You're really lost in that thing today, aren't you?"

Brody shrugged. "I've just got something on my mind that I'm trying to get out on paper."

"Let me see," Max said. He got up out of his chair and tried to take a look.

Instinctively, Brody flung the sketchbook toward his chest so that it lay facedown against his shirt. "It's not finished yet."

"Oh, come on. You're not still like that, are you?" Max ran a hand through his dark hair as he returned to his seat. "No different than you were when you were a kid."

"That's because it's a work in progress, and it isn't ready to be seen by anyone yet. If I let you look at every single line I doodled, you'd think I was a shitty artist. If I let my clients see their tats before they were finished, they'd wonder why they were paying me."

"All right. No one's attacking your talent here," Rex said in that calming way he had. It was exactly why he was Alpha. There was, of course, also the fact that he was the oldest of the Glenwoods, but everyone knew that Rex deserved his position just as much as he inherited it. "Max and I were just trying to ask who you thought might make a good third in command now that Dave is gone."

"Should've kicked him out a long time ago," Max commented. "I never did like him."

"He might not've been anyone's favorite, but you know as well as I do that Dave was given his position as a tribute for all his family had done for the pack. I can't help it if he didn't live up to the position," Rex explained.

"To say the least," Max scoffed.

Rex thumped his own chest. "Trust me, I have the most reason to be pissed at him. But I don't want to waste my time on that. I've got more important things to do, and if he's banished, then I don't have to worry about him."

Brody flipped to another clean page and attempted Robin's curves again. It was a much more palatable subject than all of this bullshit about Dave and pack politics. He ran the tip of his tongue around his teeth, knowing damn well that not a single one of them needed attention, but it was a good excuse to see her again. It might also give him a chance to study her more, to find a way to better put her luscious figure down on paper.

"He's at it again."

Brody yanked his sketchbook out of the way just before Max could snag it. "Selene's blood, what the hell do you want from me?"

"An opinion," Max growled. "We asked you who you thought would be a good third, and you didn't answer."

"That's because I don't have shit to say about it." With a sigh, Brody flipped his sketchbook shut and tucked his pencil into the binding. He eyed his two older brothers. Rex had always been a standout guy, the kind who was admired by everyone because of his position in the family and the pack. He had a temper just like any of them, but he'd quickly built himself a reputation as a credible, stable leader. He even owned a rock club to give some of his pack members jobs and a fun place to hang out. Talk about a guy who contributed his entire self to the Glenwoods.

Then there was Max, the pack's beta. He was the strong and silent type, but their parents had fallen all over him when he'd become a father. It didn't matter that Max was a single dad; he'd produced a Glenwood heir. Hunter was a great kid, and at seventeen, he was becoming more and more active in the pack. Max got all the credit for that, of course.

It wasn't any different now than when they were kids. Max had been right about that. Rex and Max were the big brothers who could do nothing wrong, and Brody had to be content to slink along in their shadows. He'd been left out of things when they were kids because he was 'too young,' which made him feel too far behind to catch up. He'd gotten involved in his own thing, and he'd made himself a successful career out of it. Most of the time, they were content to leave it at that.

So why the hell were they asking his opinion now?

"You've got to have *some* idea," Rex insisted.

"I don't know. Why don't you put everyone's

name in a hat and just draw one out?" Brody tucked his book under his arm and stood up.

"Do you really not care at all?" Max asked.

He didn't want to explain himself, but he could see how it looked. "I'm just not into politics. I care about the pack and the fact that it's run well, but that's about it. If Dave had the third position out of some obligation, then I'm sure someone else fits the bill just as well. Now if you'll excuse me, I've got something I need to do."

He made it out of the basement and up onto the first floor of the packhouse before either of his brothers had a chance to argue with him. He grabbed his keys off the kitchen counter and headed out to the garage. His Harley was there waiting for him, reminding him not only of how nice the weather was today but also the fact that it would be cold and rainy again soon enough. The power of the engine beneath him was just what he needed. The motorcycle moved quickly and smoothly underneath him, rounding curves with little more than a thought as the wind rippled through his hair. He pulled in a deep breath and let it go slowly, reveling in the freedom that came with traveling this way. It was almost as good as when he could let his wolf out and take off through the woods.

But as good as his animal form felt, it wouldn't exactly do for this errand. Brody hadn't spent much time in this part of Eugene, but he easily found the parking lot of a shopping complex with a sandwich shop, a shipping store, and several other small mom-and-pop establishments. In a new building sitting out in front of them all was Watson Dentistry. It was hard to miss, considering the massive wooden sign out front. A small electronic billboard had been mounted onto the side of the building itself, flashing photos of the doctor with his own megawatt smile and all the reasons why someone should schedule their appointment with Watson Dentistry today. The sleek, black BMW parked in the reserved spot showed that plenty of people did just that. Brody noted the license plate: 230 DOC. *What a douche.*

He wasn't in the mood for corny jokes. His wolf was already clawing to get out, and he hadn't even gone into the building yet. Robin was there, and his body knew it. He pulled in another deep breath to control it, but it wasn't the same relief he'd gotten while on his bike. She was too close now.

Grinding his jaw, he opened the front door and stepped inside. A woman with a pert nose and curly hair piled on top of her head looked up at him over her wireframes and smiled. "Hello! Can I help you?"

"Yeah. I'd like to make an appointment with Robin." Brody leaned an elbow on the counter. He'd really only intended to check the place out, to see where this mysterious woman who'd so thoroughly enraptured him worked. It would've been just as easy to call to make the appointment. Hell, he probably could've gone online and scheduled something there. But coming in meant there was a chance he'd actually see her again. He glanced around the office space through the window that looked out over the waiting room, but there was no sign of Robin.

The receptionist flicked her fingers over the keyboard of her computer. "So, you'd like to schedule a cleaning?"

"Um, no. There's really just a tooth that I need to have looked at." That was the excuse he'd given her at the shop, so he needed to stick with it.

"Ah, so you'll want to see Dr. Watson then." Her fingers flew over the keyboard once again.

"No." He thought about the man he'd seen on the electronic billboard on the side of the building and grimaced. "No, I really just want to see Robin."

The woman wore a nametag that said 'Maggie' in bold letters with a smiley face sticker after it. Maggie looked up at him. "Robin is a hygienist. You'll have to schedule a cleaning to be seen by her. She can take a look at the tooth, but Dr. Watson is the one who will actually need to diagnose the problem. I could schedule you for a cleaning with Robin, and Dr. Watson will stop in for your exam."

Tension rippled through his body. He hadn't thought this through, and now he was stuck. Hell. Whatever. As long as it meant he had a chance to see Robin again, then it didn't really matter. "Sure. That'd be fine."

"Are you a new patient?" Maggie asked, clacking away.

"Yes." And then he had to wonder if Robin had been kidding or not when she'd said they were usually booked two months in advance. If that was the case, this would be one hell of a long game to play, one he wasn't sure his wolf would tolerate for long.

Even now, as he waited for Maggie to look through the calendar, he could feel his heartbeat ramp up, a high and thready rhythm. His hearing sharpened, picking up the murmurs of the office staff as they went about their jobs, the whir of the machinery, the splash of water. He smelled the fear that a patient in a nearby exam room was exuding, tampered by the harsh scents of disinfectant and bubblegum toothpaste. Somewhere in all of that, he knew he could find Robin. Hell, if he'd been on four legs he could probably go straight to her, just following the scent of peaches.

"It looks like we actually have an opening Monday," Maggie chirped, interrupting his thoughts. "Normally, we have a much longer wait time, but we had a cancellation, so I can squeeze you in if you're good with two o'clock on Monday."

"That's fine." He wanted to leap over the counter and type it in for her, far too eager for this chance to see her. It wasn't like she'd be returning to the tattoo shop anytime soon since she'd gotten that shitty job covered up and hadn't asked about any future pieces. He'd gladly take two o'clock on Monday.

"And your name, please?"

His impatience was killing him, and he was fully aware that he'd roped himself into this. He rattled off his information as quickly as possible.

Maggie wrote his appointment on a card in loopy handwriting. "There you go. Two on Monday, with Robin and Dr. Watson." She gave him a coy look as she handed it up to him, her grin a little more than just the pleasant smile that customer service required.

"Thank you." He took the card and tucked it into

his pocket. It wasn't entirely what he'd hoped to accomplish, but it was a start.

A melodic voice caught his ear as he turned for the door. "There you are, Mr. Brooks. Maggie will get you taken care of and schedule your next appointment for you."

He whirled, not caring that the old woman in the corner chair of the waiting area was eyeing him oddly and clutching her purse. "Robin."

Those magnificent green eyes locked on his. "Brody. I wasn't expecting to see you today."

"I just figured I'd make sure you didn't have any questions about aftercare." His eyes traveled down her scrubs and landed on the spot he'd just tattooed, wishing he had a reason to lay his hands on her right now.

"I see. And do you always do your follow-ups in person?" Leaving Mr. Brooks, she came around the counter to stand in front of him.

He'd learned at a very young age how to control his wolf. It was an essential skill for a shifter unless he wanted the whole world to know just who and what he was every time his emotions started to take control. Right now, he felt as though he hadn't been trained at all. His skin prickled where fur threatened to burst through. He didn't need to see the dentist, but a searing pain ripped through his gums as he fought to hold his lupine teeth back. "Only for the clients I'm most interested in."

"Is that so?" Her pale brow arched just slightly, both an acknowledgment of his flirtation and a challenge. "Did you make an appointment?"

"I did. Maggie was happy to help me. Since you're here, though, I think I'd like to make another one." He pushed his hands into his pockets. They liked to be busy, and if he couldn't reach out to caress those soft hips of hers, he wished he could at least work on that sketch of her again. He could get it right this time, even under the harsh lighting of a dentist's office.

Now both of her brows shot up, a cute look on her. "Two appointments?"

"Actually, I wanted to see if you'd go out to dinner with me tomorrow night."

Those full lips quirked slightly as though she was thinking about it. She could say no, and he wouldn't really blame her. They didn't know each other, and he was the one who'd gone out of his way to come to her work. Then again, she was the one who'd given him her card. If they were to touch again, would that spark still be there? Brody was pretty sure he knew the answer.

"All right. Tomorrow night. You can pick me up here when I get off at seven."

"I'll do that. See you tomorrow." Turning away from her and walking back out through the front door felt like slogging through thick mud, like one of those nightmares where you need to move quickly, but your body simply won't cooperate. His wolf and his human were locked in battle, each determined to win. It wasn't until he was out of the building and there was a solid brick wall between himself and Robin that his wolf finally began to cave, though it was little relief.

He wondered what side of him would win when he took her out to dinner. It was only the next night, but it felt like an eternity.

4

Robin frowned at the bathroom mirror, thinking this light was awful for doing makeup. Either way, she swiped on an extra coat of mascara and dabbed concealer over a blemish that'd popped up along her jawline.

She'd already changed into jeans and a black top with cute, fluttery sleeves, so she turned to toss her scrubs into the office's laundry bin. Just the other day, she'd told Renee she wasn't interested in dating, yet there she was, primping for the occasion. Glancing at the scrubs in the hamper, she thought a better test of Brody might be to head out to the parking lot in her uniform, her makeup half rubbed off from wearing a mask all day, and her hair coming loose from the knot she'd worn it in. Then again, he'd already seen her at the office and hadn't balked. Points for him.

Not that she wanted to give him any points, she thought as she stepped out of the bathroom and turned off the last of the lights. She was freshly divorced. She was just doing this for fun because she could. When was the last time she actually went out on a Friday night, anyway? There was no one to stop her, and she hadn't even found a reason to stop herself. But that didn't mean it would actually turn into something. The guy was a tattoo artist, after all. He wasn't the stable, comfortable type of man she'd be looking for. *If* she were looking.

Double-checking that the autoclave was off, Robin stepped out into the waiting room. A tall, slender woman with ebony hair down to her shoulders was standing by the front desk. She held herself with grace and authority, her shoulders back and her chin lifted. Her dark eyes were full of loathing as they slid over Robin.

"May I help you?" Robin asked, instantly plugging in her customer service voice. "We're closed at the moment, but I'd be happy to take your name and number and have someone call you tomorrow to set up an appointment."

A rolling laugh escaped from her ruby lips. "As if

you could help me with anything. I'm Edith, a friend of Albert's. I'm just waiting for him."

"I see." And she did. This was just another one of her boss's rich, arrogant friends who only wanted to deal with him. Robin had never been sure what the relationships were between him and these random women, either during or after hours. She couldn't see why anyone would want to be around that asshole if they didn't have to. "Silly me! I must've had my days mixed up." Robin flashed the woman a plastic smile. "I thought he was seeing Sheila tonight. Wait, no, Brenda. Or was it Celia? Rochelle? Maybe Gloria? I don't know; you ladies are all so... similar. Anyway, you two have fun!"

As she headed out the door, she felt the woman's eyes shooting daggers at her back.

She rounded the front corner of the building toward the employee parking lot and stopped short. Brody was already there. She was glad she wouldn't have to wait around for him. She wasn't too wild about seeing him leaning against that Harley, though.

Not that he didn't look good. The tight sleeves of his t-shirt showed off his well-muscled arms, and his jeans fit his thighs perfectly before they loosened over the tops of his boots. His hair was already tousled from the ride over there, but it suited him. When his hazel eyes shot up to meet hers, Robin felt heat spread through her core.

"Hey." He slipped his phone into his back pocket and smiled. "Ready to go?"

"I thought so, but I'm not so sure about the method of transportation." Robin approached slowly, feeling his eyes on her as she studied the gleaming black metal. Her few experiences on a motorcycle had been with JC, who was always a dick of a driver in the best of circumstances. He thought it was funny to scare an inexperienced rider, and she hadn't been on one in years.

He rolled a shoulder casually. "I'll be sure to take it easy."

Her mouth opened to say no, to tell him she'd just walk home, grab her car, and then meet him wherever they were going. But her stomach had other things to say. Her gut told her she could trust him. Robin didn't understand why, but she nodded. "Okay."

Brody lifted a helmet off the back and settled it onto her head. He didn't even give her a chance to fumble with the straps. His fingers were warm and gentle under her chin as he clicked it into place and adjusted it to fit her perfectly. She still felt silly, but he didn't seem to notice.

Robin settled in behind him, realizing exactly why he'd brought a bike instead of a vehicle. It forced her to wrap her arms around his waist and press herself against his back. She felt the strength of his muscles against her and bit the inside of her cheek in appreciation. He might be an overly determined guy she'd just met, and she might not be interested in making this into anything more than a simple date, but she sure as hell would enjoy it while it lasted.

He was true to his word, navigating corners smoothly and never accelerating too fast. Robin was just starting to enjoy it when he pulled up in front of The Burger House. The building was small and unassuming, not as showy as some of the big chains, but a delectable smell was drifting through the air.

"Are burgers okay?" he asked as he reached out a hand to help her off the bike.

Her mouth was already watering. She hadn't had a burger in a while, trying to follow her doctor's recommendations. But what the hell. Robin knew she couldn't be perfect all the time, and she'd already taken a risk just by getting on the bike with him. "Sure."

The inside was warm and cozy, with pumpkin-colored walls in the dining area and a coffee bar that looked like it was homemade. An old man was at the video slots in the back corner, and a group of teenagers occupied a table near the window.

"So, this is where you take a girl when you want to impress her?" she asked when they'd ordered and had a seat.

"No. This is where I take you when I'm hungry." His smile was charming, and she had to wonder if he knew just how charming he could be.

It was working either way. "Do you come here much?"

He did that casual shoulder roll again, something that was an extension of his thoughts and obviously very natural to him. "It's as close as you can get to a homemade burger without having a family cookout. I don't always want the hassle."

"Why are you so anti-cookout?"

He laughed a little as his thumb stroked the condensation on the side of his soda. "I just have a really big family."

There was a light in his eyes when he spoke of his family, a warmth she found touching. Robin found herself wanting to know more about him. She could tell herself that this was just a bit of fun, something to shake her life up a little, as Renee would put it, but the magnetism she felt between them demanded more than that. "What's your family like?"

He lifted his brows and pursed his lips. "Huge. Close. Loud."

If he thought that would drive her away, he was mistaken. The Cassidy family might not be all that big, but they were definitely close and a bit loud. "So, what about your work? Do you come from a long line of tattoo artists?"

Brody let out a short laugh once again. "I wouldn't exactly say I went into the family business. I've always liked to draw, though, and I wanted to find a way to make a living out of it. The traditional answers would be graphic design or teaching, but tattooing was much more intriguing."

"Sure." Robin paused as their food arrived. "After all, you get paid to have women come into your booth and willingly strip down. What more could a guy ask for?"

He considered her with a mischievous look in his eyes. "Some of them aren't so willing."

"You certainly didn't mind helping," Robin pointed out, easily remembering the way he'd pulled down her leggings for her session with him.

He put his hands in the air helplessly. "The job needed to be done. Someone had to do it."

"All right, then. I'll amend my statement." She was enjoying this back-and-forth with him, chatting like they'd known each other forever. "Tattooing brings you half-naked women, whether they come in pantsless or you talk them out of those pants."

"I didn't do that with you, exactly, although I might have." His eyes raked down her body. "I still might."

"Is that so?" Had anyone ever openly wanted her like that? She licked her lips in anticipation. They were challenging each other, but Robin had a good feeling she knew exactly how it would all end.

Those gorgeous eyes bored into hers. "I guess it's really up to you. For now, we'd probably better eat before it gets cold."

"Oh." Robin looked down at the plate she'd nearly forgotten about.

Their dinner passed by swiftly, and it was a quick ride back to her place. A short date wasn't bad to start off with, but Robin didn't want it to end just yet. "Would you like to come in for a drink?"

He'd already walked her to the door—quite the gentleman for a motorcycle-riding tattoo artist—and the look in his eyes was pure velvet as he gazed down at her. "I'd love that."

Robin shut the door behind him and found herself standing far too close. Her body sensed his, measuring the distance between them as heat flushed her skin and flooded through her body. She parted her lips, knowing she should be asking him what he'd like to drink, but she couldn't even remember what she had on hand.

"I've been meaning to ask you." He stepped forward, closing the gap between them, and placed his fingers on her hips. "How's your tattoo healing up?"

"Um." Her throat had gone dry, but inside, her body was screaming for him. "I don't know. Maybe you could take a look at it for me."

"My pleasure." He held his gaze on hers as he slid his fingers across her waistband to the button of her jeans and flicked it aside.

Her chest heaved, and her heart beat loudly in her ears. Robin had been mortified when he'd done this before, caught off-guard and self-conscious, but she could see the desire in his eyes and feel it in his fingertips as they traced along the very top of her panties, tugging them down ever so gently and just where he knew the tattoo to be.

Brody looked down as his touch glided over her. "It's healing beautifully, but I'd expect that on such a perfect canvas."

When those eyes flicked back to hers, she was undone. Their mouths came together, softly at first and then more demanding as they explored each other. The feel of his tongue against hers sent the same sizzling energy through her body as his fingers on her bare skin did, and she pressed her hands against his back. Robin felt the long lines of hard muscle leading up to those wide shoulders and raked her fingers upward through the back of his hair.

His moan vibrated in her mouth as he plunged his hands inside the open waistband of her jeans. His fingers roved over her curves, cradling handfuls of her hips and buttocks.

Robin moved backward, knowing the way without having to look up from what she was doing. She skirted the side table near the front door as she clutched at the hem of his shirt and pulled it over his head, leaving it draped over her purse. She backed into the hall as he thumbed open her blouse, sliding it off her shoulders. Somewhere along the way, she stepped out of her shoes and kicked them aside, hearing the echoing thumps as he did the same.

Her bedroom was only dimly lit by the overhead light in the living room, but it was enough for her to appreciate the hardness of his body as they tumbled onto the bed. His arms were thick and muscled, his chest wide. The man might be an artist, but he had the body of a lumberjack.

He stripped off her jeans and flung them aside before tracing his kisses down her throat to the swell of her breasts. She moaned softly when he dipped his tongue inside the lacy material to tease her nipple. Robin let out a breath as he sent yet another wave of heat through her body.

Letting her hands roam, Robin felt the stiffness of his bulge through his jeans. His obvious need for her sent waves pulsing through her blood as she released him from the last of his clothes and took his hard member into her palm. His breath shivered with every stroke, escalating her need for him. She pressed him against her entrance as his mouth left her breast to return to her lips, and a gasp of pleasure escaped her as they converged.

Robin reeled at the way he felt inside her, moving, rocking, coaxing, throbbing. Power and pleasure rippled through her body. Tingles of energy converged with those ripples as his chest hair brushed against her nipples. The way he touched her and kissed her, so gentle yet so full of craving, made her feel like a goddess. Her body clenched around him, then burst into spasms of ecstasy, urging on his own pleasure as rapture overtook them.

She smiled as she lay panting in his arms. Yes, Brody had definitely shaken things up a little.

5

QUICK ON YOUR FEET. GOOD. NICE DODGE! BRODY'S hackles rose with pride as he watched his nephew move with agility. He observed carefully, analyzing Hunter's every movement, ready to give feedback that would help him fight should the need arise. If he turned away from his foe before the battle was over or exposed any vulnerability, he would need to work on it.

Their packmate Conner's teeth snapped viciously, just barely missing the fur on Hunter's rump as he danced away over the flat rock they'd chosen as their battleground.

Hoo hoo hoo! Can't get me, loser! Hunter teased.

The younger packmates could learn plenty of lessons from him, but Brody knew they needed to learn some on their own. Brody watched the look in Conner's eyes shift, and he knew that Hunter was about to do just that.

Wanna bet? With a swiftness that rivaled Hunter's, Conner lowered his furry head and charged. His shoulder rammed right into Hunter's side as the younger wolf was busy gloating, sending him sprawling off the rock and into the dirt and leaves surrounding it.

The other young wolves who'd gathered to watch were yipping with excitement over the upheaval.

Hey, that's cheating! Hunter was smaller and more nimble, and it only took a moment before he was on his paws again and charging up onto the rock.

No, it's not. Brody stepped quickly between them, giving his nephew a stern look. *You're quick, and that's a distinct advantage for you, but it doesn't mean you're impervious. You should all know your strengths and weaknesses; sometimes, they can be the same thing.*

Hunter looked around Brody, no longer snarling but obviously still pissed. *It's not my fault he plays college football. Of course he'd tackle me like that.*

Yeah, and it worked, too. Conner was proudly standing his ground, clearly pleased with himself but trying not to boast.

The muscles in Brody's face twitched. They

might all look like wolves, but they were still young men. He liked seeing how they'd grown over the years, watching them build their confidence and learning to rein it in just enough. It was something he'd been missing in his life for a while. Hell, Devin would be just about as old as some of these boys now. No, not boys. Young men. It tugged at his heart, but he shook it off when he saw how much everyone was reacting to the round that'd just ended.

All right. I think that's about enough for today.

Grumbling growls sounded through the air.

I want a rematch, Hunter insisted.

Anytime, Conner replied.

No. Next time, Brody corrected. He pulled his human form back to the surface. The cool breeze rippled through his fur as it retreated, and he felt as much as heard the faint cracking in his skull as his muzzle flattened and returned to a human shape. He looked around as the rest of them did the same. It would be much easier to keep them all in check this way without everyone's thoughts echoing through his mind.

"I know everyone feels like they have something to prove," he began, eyeing the last two contenders, "but this isn't about who beats who out here. Our pack might be more traditional than some, but we're not so old-fashioned that we fight for sheer power."

And if they were, he noted, Hunter would be getting a run for his money. If Rex never had kids, he could become Alpha one day. Brody knew that was exactly why Hunter was so confident in himself— and why he was so butthurt that Conner had managed to beat him. The fact that Conner hadn't even known he was a wolf until his teenage years probably didn't help, either.

"At some point, we very well may need to fight, but not each other. It's my job to make sure you know what the hell you're doing so you don't get creamed out there. So like I said, know your strengths and weaknesses and work on them. Don't get cocky. And no sparring behind my back."

There were more groans and grumbles, but Brody knew they would obey. He'd find out about it as soon as it happened, and that would take all the fun out of their training sessions.

Some of the young wolves quickly shifted back to their four-legged forms and streamed off through the woods as they headed home or elsewhere, but Hunter and Conner flanked Brody as he moved toward the trail.

"That was quite the little speech," Hunter began.

Conner nodded. "And you let us spar a lot longer than you usually do."

"We had the time," Brody replied.

The boys glanced at each other.

Inwardly, Brody wanted to grin. They were solid enemies when they practiced their fighting skills, but they were packmates and family any other time. That was just as it should be, and he liked to think he had something to do with it.

"I don't know," Hunter hedged. "I think he seems kind of chipper today. For an old fart."

"Yep. He ought to be at home warming his bones by the fire with a warm mug of milk, thinking about bedtime," Conner agreed.

Stopping on the trail, Brody rounded on them. "Would you rather I take the two of you on instead?"

"You don't have to. As long as you tell us why you've been grinning like a fool all morning." Hunter cocked an eyebrow.

"Might have something to do with the fact that you got in so late last night."

Brody sighed. He'd been thinking about Robin all day, but he hadn't realized that he'd actually let it show. "Why do you *think*?"

"Ha! I told you that was it!" Hunter gave Conner a shove in the arm.

"No, I told *you*. It's not like you have any experience in the pussy department." He shoved Hunter back.

"The hell I don't!"

"Turn down the testosterone already," Brody said with a laugh. "Yes, I was out with a woman last night, not that either one of you knows a damn thing about it."

"Who was it?" Conner asked. "Anyone we know?"

"I highly doubt it." Robin was human; that much Brody had known instantly. That didn't mean she couldn't have mingled with the Glenwood pack at some point. After all, there were shifters all over Eugene. Most humans had met them at one time or another. "She works for a dental office, so she's probably never seen the likes of you."

"Is she hot?" Hunter pressed.

Brody could see the excitement in Hunter's eyes, though he knew his definition of hot probably wasn't anything close to his nephew's. Robin was incredibly hot; his temperature rose at the mere thought of her after feeling her sweet naked curves pressed against his body. She was a woman who knew what she wanted and what she was doing, and he hoped she had a chance to show him that again sometime soon. Very soon. "Definitely."

He turned and started walking down the path again while the boys ribbed each other about their romantic pursuits—or lack thereof. Brody couldn't help but smile when he thought about Robin. She was pure torture when she was near, bringing his wolf simmering to the surface and threatening to boil over. He hadn't felt that out of control since he was younger than Hunter, when a pretty girl could make a bit of fur emerge from the back of his neck. But his beast would never have truly come forward without his bidding.

With Robin, it was different. In a way, he was surprised he'd made it through tattooing her without completely losing his cool. Even so, he'd wanted to find whoever that JC asshole was and destroy him for marking her like that. When he'd gone to Watson Dentistry to make his appointment, he'd known Robin was in the building not just because it was likely, but because he'd *felt* it.

And the scene the two of them had created in her bedroom last night? Hell, he never could've prayed to Selene for something that magnificent.

She was like his fantasies come true, which was still almost too good to believe.

His mind, as it often did, drifted back to his art. Robin was inevitably mixed in with those thoughts. He'd tried to sketch his muse, and he'd only been left with fodder for the recycling bin. But that'd been when he'd tried to capture her the way she'd looked at the shop: standing in the doorway, beautiful, yet uncertain.

The key was to recreate her in the way he knew her now: lying on a bed, the sheets rumpled around her curves, hiding just enough to keep a bit of her modesty. Her eyes, lazy with the satisfaction of what they'd just done. Her lips, full from kissing him, yet ready to taste more. Her fingers, curved and relaxed where she'd flung her hands out on either side of her.

He could hear Hunter and Conner behind him, still razzing each other. The poor kids had no idea what was in store for them when they fell for someone for more than a nice rack or pretty eyes.

Shit. Right away, Brody had known this was more than simple attraction. It was an irresistible pull, one he'd recognized even though he hadn't felt it before. Still, this was the first time he'd admitted it to himself, and it hit harder than he'd imagined.

Robin was his mate.

"Hey." Hunter's heavy footsteps galloped behind him as he caught up. "Are you going to the meeting Monday?"

"Nope."

"But you missed the last one," Hunter pointed out.

Brody gave him a playful knock on the arm. "Already trying to boss everyone around, aren't you?"

Hunter's face was sour for a moment, but he quickly recovered. "I was just asking."

Once again, Brody felt that familiar tug at his heart. At this point in his life, Hunter was as close to a son as he would ever get. Brody had been there for him in as many ways as he knew how, but maybe he was still failing him. "I'll make the next one. I've got an appointment."

"An appointment where?" Conner asked suspiciously.

"Can't a guy keep his own schedule?" Brody grinned. "I have a dentist appointment, if you must know."

The two young men stared at him in stunned silence for a moment before they burst out in laughter. They knew, just as well as Brody, that shifters had zero need for dentists.

"More like an appointment with your friend with benefits," Conner joked.

Hunter chuckled. "Hey, I'm just glad to hear you can still get it up."

The two of them carried on behind him, and Brody just shook his head. They had no idea.

6

"Do you mind if I have mint instead of my usual bubblegum polish today, dear? I have a date down at the senior center this afternoon." She leaned closer to Robin and touched her arm with her wrinkled hand. "You never know where it might lead," she added with a wink.

"How exciting, Mrs. Jenkins! Sure, let me get that for you." Robin hummed behind her mask as she finished up with her patient, knowing Mrs. Jenkins wasn't the only one getting some action. She'd been on the moon ever since that night with Brody. Holy hell. He'd looked great with his clothes on, but even better with them off. Brody had moved his hands over her body not just with lust, but appreciation, as though he were trying to memorize every curve. She couldn't remember the last time she'd felt so desired.

She'd get to see him again later that day. Robin had never slept with one of her patients before, and the thought made her want to giggle like a teenager.

Her warm, fuzzy mood cracked around the edges when Dr. Watson appeared in the doorway. His dazzling white veneers were blinding under the harsh light of the office. He had a tendency to flash them in a mock smile every time someone looked at him, though the sentiment never reached his eyes. She'd wondered if that was from all the Botox or just his horrid personality. "Robin, you'll need to take a late lunch. Thaddeus Elmington is coming in for a cleaning."

Robin was glad she still had her mask on so her boss wouldn't see her expression. For one thing, he shouldn't be discussing that information in front of other patients, even if it was only the person's name. The name, of course, was the only part that mattered to Dr. Watson. Thaddeus Elmington was a hotshot lawyer from a family that was absolutely loaded with old timber money. It was a feather in Dr. Watson's cap to have him as a regular patient; therefore, the man was allowed in at any time, whether there was room in the schedule for him or not.

"I would, but it's going to shorten my time for my afternoon appointments." And those appointments were particularly important today.

He lifted his chin slightly. "You can find a way to manage it." Before she could argue with him any further, he'd moved off down the hallway.

Finished with Mrs. Jenkins, Robin walked her patient up to the front. Maggie caught her eye and arched a brow, wanting to talk. Having a few minutes before her next appointment—a luxury she definitely wouldn't have that afternoon—Robin stuck around the front desk and poked through some paperwork until Mrs. Jenkins had been scheduled for her next appointment and was out the door.

Moments later, her sister Renee stepped into the waiting room and waved at Robin through the glass divider at the front desk. Robin motioned for her to join her back in the patient checkout area.

"Remind me never to eat Mom's peanut brittle again," Renee groaned. "I can't believe I broke my tooth and have to get a damn crown!"

Robin laughed. "That's the most expensive peanut brittle you'll ever eat."

"Never again."

When Mrs. Jenkins was gone, Maggie whirled in

her chair toward the sisters with her eyes bright. "So, how did it go with the hot tattoo artist?"

"Come on, spill the tea," Renee added. "I hate that phrase, but that's what Kennedy says all the time."

It was impossible not to smile. When was the last time Robin had gotten to gossip about a first date? "It was pretty great, actually. He's got a motorcycle, which scared the hell out of me at first. He took me to a burger place."

"Burgers?" Renee cocked a brow. "That doesn't sound very romantic."

Robin shook her head as she thought about the easy companionship between them as they'd sat together at The Burger House. "I wouldn't have thought so, either, but it actually kind of was. It was different, but I guess that's one of the things I like about Brody."

"He sure as hell was determined to see you when he came in here to schedule his appointment," Maggie noted. "I don't think I've ever known a man willing to make a dentist appointment just to see a woman. Oh, wait. That's today, isn't it?"

Robin had sat in one of the other available chairs, and now she sagged against the back of it. She glanced at the office doorway before she leaned forward. "Yes, but Watson just told me I have to squeeze in another appointment for his *friend*."

Maggie's mouth went slack. "I just told him there was no room in the schedule. He already made me overbook a spot on Friday for another one of his friend's veneers. I'm going to have a whole waiting room full of pissed off patients pushed well past their appointment times."

"If it means he gets to rub elbows with the upper class of Eugene, he won't give a shit," Robin noted. "You should've seen him preening while he tossed that guy's name around."

"He might as well plaster it all over that tacky billboard outside," Renee added.

"He doesn't have to when he spends his weekends flying all those snobs up to Lake Oswego to play golf," Maggie reminded her. "Then he's all over social media, ever so casually mentioning his private plane and all the big names who've been in it. I mean, really, these people need fillings and root canals just like the rest of us. I don't get what it is with him."

"He's probably just insecure and needs to surround himself with rich people to project an image and feel better about his miserable life," Robin speculated.

"Speaking of insecure, the man's in his sixties," Renee noted. "There's no way he can look like that naturally. He's got to be going to one of those 'spas' or something."

Maggie pulled a pencil out of the curly bun on top of her head and twiddled it between her fingers. "Maybe a little nip here and a tuck there?"

"Something," Robin uttered. His hair was too dark and thick, and his skin was as smooth as a baby's bottom. It was well done, considering she couldn't spot any evidential scarring, but she knew something had to be happening.

Barb, Watson's assistant, appeared. "Hi, Renee. I'll take you back and get you seated."

"Have fun," Robin teased, her sister flipping her the bird as she followed Barb down the hallway.

The little bell over the front door dinged, and Robin and Maggie turned as a woman with a pinched face slowly sauntered through the waiting room. She carried her designer purse looped over one arm, and she glanced around as though she wasn't sure she was in the right place. Robin recognized Christina Harding. Her husband was some sort of producer, Robin thought. Christina was a stay-at-home wife, but she kept herself busy by getting drunk and crashing her little sports cars. She stepped up to the counter. "I need to see Albert, please."

Robin cringed. She hated it when his favorite patients referred to him by his first name when he'd made it very clear to the staff that they were never to call him anything but Dr. Watson. He insisted it was about being professional, but Robin knew it was more about his superiority complex.

Maggie, always quick as lightning on the computer, checked the schedule. Robin knew Maggie didn't even need to consult the computer, because she usually had most of the day's appointments memorized. "It looks like I could get you in on Monday."

Lines from years of smoking radiated from Christina's mouth, and they deepened as she pursed her lips. "I meant that I need to see him today."

"Why don't you have a seat for a moment, and I'll see what I can do." Maggie suggested pleasantly. As soon as she was out of Christina's line of sight, she turned to Robin and made a face. They both knew what she was there for, and they didn't like it.

A beeping noise blared from the TV in the waiting room. The placid daytime programming was interrupted as the view switched to a news anchor. "We're here to bring you breaking news. The body of a young woman has been found in Spencer Butte Park by a pair of hikers. Police have yet to identify the victim. Speculation is mounting quickly that it could be Alissa Grainger, another hiker who went missing last week, but there is no confirmation just yet. We'll bring you the latest news as soon as it comes in. We've reached out to the police department and the parks service for further comment, but —" The picture blinked out and turned black.

Dr. Watson was standing behind them with the remote. He showed his veneers once again, but this time, it wasn't in the context of a smile. "You have jobs to do, ladies. I don't pay you to sit around and watch the news."

Robin stood from her chair and felt Watson's eyes on her backside as she turned to head back to her operatory.

"Robin, you know I include a gym membership in your benefits package."

Robin's mouth fell open for a moment as she froze, looking for an answer. She was used to Dr. Watson being condescending, but she didn't think he'd ever been so directly insulting. "I can always lose weight. But all the money in the world won't fill the void in that cold, shallow soul of yours."

The words escaped her lips before she could

even think about them, but the doctor hadn't seemed to hear them, already moving on to something he cared about more. He'd spotted one of his favorite patients in the waiting room and immediately went out to greet her with open arms. "Christina! How are you today, darling?" Dr. Watson gave her a light embrace and a peck on the cheek.

"Not well, I'm afraid." She pouted up at him. The woman was nearly as old as he was, and she should've been well beyond pouting. She gently touched the side of her face. "I'm in an awful lot of pain with this tooth that keeps bothering me every now and then. Your girl said you wouldn't be able to get me in until Monday."

"Don't you worry. I'll make sure you're taken care of. Why don't you come on back with me for a minute?" Taking her by the hand, he led Christina to his private office. She emerged a minute later with a small square of white paper in her hand and a smile on her face. She didn't bother to say goodbye to Maggie or make sure she could secure that appointment for Monday.

Robin and Maggie exchanged a long look and then went back to work. As Robin returned to her exam room to disinfect before the next patient arrived, she felt tension creeping through the muscles of her shoulders. There were plenty of legitimate prescriptions written in this office, ones that went through the computer system and could be quickly tied back to the examinations performed and the results thereof. These little favors that 'Albert' did for his friends, however, were always conveniently written by hand. It would take some investigating on behalf of a state agency to prove he was doing anything wrong, and she was sure as shit that none of those special patients were going to rat him out. Even if Robin could become a whistleblower and nail him to the wall, that would mean she'd lose the only job in the area she was qualified for that paid well enough to keep a roof over her head. God knows how expensive homes were in Eugene, and Robin had worked hard to buy her little bungalow. It put her between a rock and a hard place. Her only solace was knowing that karma's a bitch. It would all catch up with the bastard someday.

She turned her mind back to Brody as she wiped down the chair and changed the plastic cover over the computer keyboard. He kept her thoughts active in a completely different way. She was just as unsure about him as she was with her work life, but it wasn't the same. At least while she was figuring it out, she was going to enjoy the hell out of herself. Any man who willingly and purposefully gave her that much pleasure was worth spending time with.

She was smiling by the time the notification flashed on her computer screen, telling her the next patient had arrived. Robin headed out to the waiting room, both excited and nervous about the appointment that was yet to come.

7

BRODY JIGGLED HIS KNEE AS HE SAT IMPATIENTLY IN the waiting room. He drummed his fingers on the arm of the chair, but it didn't help. He needed something to do, something to keep him in check, and the bland home renovation show on the TV wasn't cutting it. Maggie had given him a sly smile when he'd checked in, making Brody wonder just what Robin might've told her. At least she was smiling, so that was probably a good sign.

Not that he really had any reason to wonder. The state of satisfaction he'd been in as he'd pulled her body against his was undeniable. His wolf had been able to sense that same feeling within her. Plus, he had eyes. Robin had looked at him with a glowing contentment, something he knew he could take pride in.

The door opened, and Robin appeared in her scrubs. She'd changed out of them for their date, he knew, and he noted just how gorgeous those green eyes of hers looked in contrast to the deep purple fabric. "Brody?" she called, just as she would for any other patient.

But when he stood and their eyes locked, he knew she wasn't looking at him like any other patient. Her mouth curved upward in a sensual smile, and he felt a ripple of heat through his body. Maybe it'd been a mistake to take her out before this appointment because it was going to be hard to keep this professional.

"I'll take you right back here for your x-rays." She led the way through the winding hall and into a room tucked into the back. "You can have a seat right there, and then you get to wear this sexy lead apron."

Her hands fluttered gently near his neck as she placed the protective apron over him, and his wolf instantly clawed against the underside of his skin. Being together in her bed had calmed it briefly, but apparently, that would only last so long. "So, come here often?"

"Just about every day," she said with a smile as

she set up the machine, "unless I happen to be across town getting a tattoo. There's this guy that comes highly recommended, especially because he's so good at following up with his clients to make sure they're healing well. I just can't quite remember his name."

"I think I know who you're talking about. I heard he has a thing for strawberry blondes." She'd straightened her hair that day, the soft waves falling in a crisp line along her jaw. He wanted to reach out and run his finger over that line, to memorize it and save it for later.

"Hold still."

When she was done snapping a series of x-rays, he followed her past a surprising number of other exam rooms to hers at the front of the building. A wide window looked out onto the landscaping surrounding the office. Most of it was what he'd expect from a dental office, with cool gray walls and bright white flooring, but he noted several framed photos of her family dotting the walls amongst posters about oral cancer and the importance of flossing daily. It only told him a little about her, and he found himself wanting to know even more.

"Have a seat." She gestured at the patient chair,

scanned over his medical history form, and clipped
a bib around his neck.

Again with those soft hands so close to him,
Brody felt his wolf rising inside him. This was going
to be one long-ass appointment. He wanted to know
everything about her, but he was pretty damn sure
she wasn't ready to know all about him. "I see. You
bring me in here, all alone, and lay me back on this
chair. I think I know exactly what's happening."

"It's only fair, right? I believe you had me in a
rather similar position less than a week ago. At least
I don't have to pull your pants down to do my job.
Probably. Maybe." She smiled mischievously at him
as she turned to the computer.

The sweet, peachy smell drifted across his
nostrils as she moved her arm to type something in,
and a tightness took over his stomach and further
down. It would be so easy to reach over, drag her
onto his lap, capture her mouth with his, and take
her all over again. Damn, this was difficult!

"All right. Let's take a peek at those x-rays." There
was a moment of silence before she looked back at
him. "What tooth was bothering you again?
According to these x-rays, you've got the most
perfect teeth I've ever seen."

He'd known she would catch him in that lie, but

he wasn't sure he cared now. He was there with her; at the moment, that was all that really mattered. "It was a great excuse to make sure I could see you again, wasn't it?"

"Really?" She narrowed her eyes, but the corners of her mouth were still curled up. The words hung between them for one long, painful moment in which Brody couldn't tell how she'd react. Until she burst out laughing so hard that she ended up bent over on her stool with her elbows braced on her knees. Tears were in her eyes when she finally straightened up again. "Brody, what the hell am I going to do with you?"

"Drag me back to your place so you can take advantage of me? Or you could just shut the door. That would work, too." He grinned, knowing even without asking that she wasn't the kind of woman who'd risk her job like that. Still, it was fun to think about.

"How about I just clean your teeth since you're here?" She pulled her mask up and laid the chair back.

He couldn't really flirt with her anymore with her hands in his mouth, but Brody didn't mind. It still meant that he got to be close to her, which was the point of this appointment in the first place. He studied the careful, focused look in her green eyes as she looked over his teeth and gums with that ridiculously tiny mirror and relished the way her breasts occasionally brushed against his head.

Too soon, it was time for Dr. Watson to come in. He strutted into the room and snapped on his gloves. "All right. Let's see what we've got here. I understand there's a tooth that's bothering you?"

"I think that was just a mistake in the system," Robin volunteered. "Everything looks fine to me."

"I'll be the judge of that," the doctor snapped as he peered into Brody's mouth.

Anger flooded through Brody's veins, but confusion took over when he saw the doctor's face. He had the stiff, overly-taut look of someone who'd been fighting the signs of aging. His own parents were older than this man, he was sure. Joan and Jimmy Glenwood were young wolves at heart, but they'd let their hair go gray when it was time and didn't mind the extra lines on their faces.

Watson was quick with his exam and soon leaned back. "I don't think there's much to see here. Keep brushing and flossing like you've been, and stay away from candy and soda. Do you have any questions?"

"No." He just wanted this prick to get the hell out of there so he could be alone with Robin again.

Dr. Watson pulled off his gloves. "Robin, did you tell Maggie to move Thaddeus Elmington's appointment?"

Brody's gaze snapped to Robin just in time to see her eyes harden into emeralds. "Not exactly. She and I were discussing the best way to coordinate the schedule to accommodate him without shortening the other appointments."

"That's not up to you. I told you what I needed you to do, and I expect it to be done," Watson barked.

If he thought it was hard to hold his wolf back when he was near Robin, it was nearly impossible now. Brody's muscles reacted with the speed of his animal counterpart as he launched himself into a seated position. "What the hell makes you think you can talk to her that way?"

The doctor's eyes widened as he scooted back quickly on the stool. "Excuse me?"

"It seems to me that she does an awful lot for you around here, and you ought to treat her better. If you do have a problem with her, you sure as shit don't need to be airing it out in front of your patients. Have some goddamn decency and respect." Brody's legs twitched as he considered jumping to his feet and pounding this guy into the wall like he deserved.

Though he obviously had zero awareness of how he affected his staff, Dr. Watson definitely noticed the rage seething inside of Brody. "My apologies," he mumbled to Robin before slinking out of the room.

Her tongue was pressed against the inside of her cheek as she slowly returned to the stool. Robin glanced out the door. "You didn't have to do that," she said quietly.

"I'm sorry." Brody doubted Dr. Watson's apology had been genuine, but his own was. "I probably overreacted, but if he were my boss, I'd have a hard time not slugging those fucking Chiclets out of his mouth. He's a full-blown, top-shelf douche."

A snort of laughter escaped from behind her mask. "That's not fair."

"What? You don't agree?"

"I do. I just wish I could call him that myself. Let's get things finished up." Robin pulled on a pair of new gloves.

"Maybe I didn't need to call him out for the way he treated you, but you didn't have to make excuses for me coming in here without a cavity or anything," he noted as he lay back again.

She took a long piece of floss from the tray nearby and began her work, expertly threading it between his teeth. Robin spoke quietly. "I guess I didn't, but it seemed easier than trying to explain it all. You've only gotten a small taste of what Dr. Watson's like. He'd probably have more to say to me if he thought I was using my job to get dates." She muttered something under her breath that he couldn't quite hear.

He picked up on the scent of peaches again, and every muscle in his body was tense. Brody felt an aching in his bones as he fought to keep them where they were. Many changes happened when he shifted, and keeping everything in check was getting more and more difficult. First, he had to be this close to Robin in a public setting that also felt incredibly intimate, with her face so close to his and his head practically in her lap. That was hard enough, considering the night they'd shared, but then Dr. Watson had kicked his protective instincts into overdrive. The man had no idea how lucky he was that Brody had the control he did, though it probably looked like he didn't. Brody's breathing increased as he felt his beast pushing once again, demanding to come out. He just had a little while longer. He had to keep it in check, but he felt a jolt of adrenaline run through his system as he realized he might not be able to do that.

Robin, meanwhile, had no idea what he was going through and was still talking. "Your x-rays really are quite remarkable, by the way." She turned away from her work to squint at the computer screen again.

All the training and years of experience simply couldn't compete with the emotions churning inside him. A stinging sensation shot through his gums as his fangs burst forward.

And pierced right through the material of her glove.

"Ow!" Robin jumped back and stared at her pointer finger, her eyes wide with shock. "What the hell?"

Brody had been fighting so hard against that damn wolf, and now was the moment it chose to finally settle down. It retreated swiftly and left him alone to deal with this. His throat tightened as he tried to think of something to say. How could he explain?

"That's weird. I don't know how, but I must've nicked myself against your tooth while flossing." Robin was still staring at the speck of blood, bright against her blue glove. "I guess you've got some pretty sharp teeth in there."

"I'm so sorry." He moved to sit up. Holy hell, he'd fucked up. Bad.

"Oh, don't worry about it. It was just a freak accident." She quickly raised his chair and pulled her glove off. She crossed to the sink and began disinfecting the wound. "Standard procedure is that we both need to be tested. We'll basically treat this like a needle-stick. We have to check for HIV, hepatitis, things like that. I don't mean that as any sort of insult to you. I'm sorry for the trouble; it's just the way things have to be done."

"Really, don't apologize." Especially since it wasn't her fault. "I'm fully aware of the protocol. It's the same for me in the tattoo industry, so I get it. I can guarantee you that I'm clear in that department, but I'll get tested this afternoon. My sister's a nurse, so I've got an in."

She nodded, but she was still staring at her hand as though it had six fingers instead of five. The sweet flush of her skin had gone pale.

He had to tell her. There were far more implications than she realized, but he couldn't just tell her now. She was freaked out enough, and the middle of a busy dental office just wasn't the place. "Listen, to show you just how not sorry you need to be, why don't you come to my place for dinner tonight? I'll text you the address."

"Um, sure. I'll let you check out with Maggie if that's okay. I've got to get this taken care of." She stepped out of the exam room.

Brody had swung his legs over the side of the chair, and he pressed his hand to his forehead. This was going to be a tough one to explain, both to Robin and his pack. Shit. Shit, shit, shit.

"Dr. Watson, I need to talk to you." Her voice drifted in through the open door.

"I'm busy."

"This is important. I've had a blood exposure. I'm canceling the last of my appointments for the day so I can get to the lab before they close." Brody could still hear the fear in her voice. Not, he was sure, because she was worried that he had some disease, but because the incident had happened at all. She seemed like the type who liked everything to go according to plan, and this sure as hell hadn't been scheduled into her day.

"Are you kidding me?" Dr. Watson's ire was thick, and Brody heard the slapping sound of papers hitting a desk. "I've already had to rearrange the afternoon's schedule because you insisted on screwing it up. Elmington is thoroughly insulted, and now you're costing me money because you've got to go and get tested. Shit, Robin."

"I'm sorry, Dr. Watson."

His wolf had already tried its best to surface, and now it was so close, he thought it very well might come surging out of him as he shot off the exam chair. Brody curled his fists as he marched out of the exam room. It only took a quick turn of his head to see Dr. Watson in his lavish office. He stood behind a large wooden desk, his teeth bared and his hands on his hips. Robin was in front of him with her back to Brody.

The next thing he knew, Brody was standing next to her. "How can you give zero fucks about the well-being of your employees and still be in business? Robin just told you she had a blood exposure."

Caution rippled through Watson's eyes, but he pointed toward the door. "This really isn't any of your business."

"Considering I'm the person on the other end of this little problem, it's very much my business."

"This is all getting out of hand—"

"Yeah, that's exactly my point," Brody countered. "In dental school, was there a special class on how to be cruel to your staff and rude to your patients? Because I'm damn sure you aced it."

Anger simmered under Dr. Watson's stiff face, but Brody was sure he smelled fear mixed with it. "Robin, go to the lab. You, sir, need to get out of my office. You're not welcome as a patient here anymore."

"Trust me, that's not a problem." Brody looked down at Robin, saw the slight nod of her chin, and headed out to the waiting room. He passed a wide-eyed Maggie on the way, who had a hand pressed over her mouth. She might've been hiding her shock or her laughter; he wasn't sure. He burst out into the waiting room, pissed that this had gone the way it had.

The young woman waiting in a chair near the water cooler looked up at him, and recognition sparked in her eyes. He knew people by their tattoos better than their faces, and he quickly spotted the recent piece on her calf. He couldn't remember her name, but he definitely remembered her. She'd told him all about the baby raccoon she'd rescued after it fell down in the wall of her parents' house and how she'd adopted it when the mother wouldn't take it back. "Hey."

"Hey. How are you?" Her eyes darted toward the

back, realizing that she already knew things weren't the best.

"Fine," he lied. "How's it healing up?"

The woman turned her leg so that he could see it better. "Pretty well, I think. I'm already getting lots of compliments on it."

It looked fine to him, and he gave her a nod. "Great. Come and see me when you're ready for the next one. And in the meantime, you might want to find a new dentist. This one's a raging asshole."

Maggie called out to the young woman. "The doctor's ready to see you, miss."

"Wish me luck," the woman said to Brody as she stood and gathered her purse.

"You'll need it." Brody headed out the door, wondering how the hell he was going to tell Robin the truth.

8

MOST OF THE SHAKING HAD STOPPED IN ROBIN'S bones by the time she pulled up in front of the address Brody had given her later that evening. The walkway skirted the wide garage at the front and led to a heavy wooden door with a stained glass window perched at its top. A shadow moved behind it as she lifted her hand to knock, and it opened to reveal Brody. The frayed ends of his jeans brushed the tops of his bare feet. He was casual in a pocket tee, the drab green of it grabbing the color of his eyes.

"Hey. I'm glad you came." He opened the door wider to let her in.

The afternoon had been so busy that she hadn't spent much time speculating what sort of a place Brody had. Now that she could see it, it was decidedly him. The warm gold on three walls of the living room picked up the hickory of the floor. An Eames chair relaxed just in front of the bay window and faced the fireplace, where the light would be best for using the pencils and sketchbook on the side table. Several canvases adorned the deep red accent wall behind the fireplace, most of which she figured were his work. A wide doorway led to the kitchen, the granite countertops dark against the honey-colored cabinets. The place was clean and minimal but warm and inviting, just like him.

"Me, too. I'd really like to talk to you about today."

He twitched his shoulder. "Mind if we do it in the kitchen? I've got to finish up dinner."

"So, you can cook?" Robin asked as she followed him. "I wasn't sure if this would be another burger date."

"I cook," he said with a smile. "Is it that much of a surprise? Help yourself to anything you'd like in the fridge."

Robin opened the stainless-steel door to find an assortment of cans. She grabbed a sparkling water, thinking about the horrible meals her ex had made. She was convinced he'd done it just so she'd never ask him to cook again. "Not everyone likes to spend time in the kitchen, despite how many people have started their own cooking shows on the internet these days."

"The worst are the ones where you think it's a regular cooking video, then you realize the person is wearing nothing but an apron. Kind of disappointing when you were only there for the recipe."

Robin laughed, glad she hadn't yet taken a sip of her water, and perched herself on a barstool at the island. "Is there anything I can do to help?"

Brody took the lid off a small pot of rice and poked a fork down into it. "No, I think I've got everything taken care of. I should've asked if you were allergic to anything. We really don't need two medical incidents in one day."

"I'm glad you're not being weird about this whole thing, and I really am sorry," she began. Her mind had been occupied all afternoon with the myriad of ways she could make it up to him. "I must've been so distracted because nothing like that has ever happened to me before."

He glanced at her as he poured oil into a wok and turned on the flame beneath it. "I told you there was no reason to apologize."

"Most patients wouldn't handle it the way you are." She could just imagine what a fit Thaddeus

Elmington or Christina Harding would've thrown if she'd told them they'd need to go for testing.

He tossed his hair. "I'm not like other guys."

She laughed at the joke, even though she knew it was true. "I guess you really aren't. Did everything go okay with your test? You said your sister would be able to help you with that."

"Not a problem at all." Deftly handling a pair of extra-long chopsticks, Brody quickly scrambled a couple of eggs in the bottom of the wok. Those came out, and neatly cut strips of marinated beef went in next. A delectable scent immediately filled the kitchen.

"I know it'll be a couple of days until we get our results back, but I'll be sure to let you know as soon as I have mine."

"I'll do the same. I don't think we have anything to worry about, though." Brody had lines around his eyes, the kind that came not only with age, but from studying his art so closely. They deepened now as he focused on the meal he was making, easily flicking the beef in the pan until it was mostly cooked and then putting it back in the marinade.

Robin pulled in a breath but kept herself from sighing. She really liked Brody, more than she wanted to admit. He was just a random guy who happened to give her a tattoo, and she wouldn't have met him at all if Poppy hadn't gotten behind on her schedule. She'd noticed the connection between them immediately, a link that felt as though it'd always been there. As nice as it was, it made her realize that a chasm had opened between them, a distance she was unsure how to cross. All she could do was try.

"I think I should also apologize for Dr. Watson's behavior," she began.

He set his metal spatula down on the counter with a thunk and turned to her, his eyes blazing. "How can you possibly work for someone like that, anyway?"

Robin blinked. "I know he's terrible, but the paycheck keeps me coming to work every day. Now that I'm single, I have to pay for my mortgage and everything else on one salary. Watson brings in a ton of clients—though I'm really not sure why—and plenty of them are rolling in money. Between insurance and private payments, he can actually afford to give us decent pay without thinking he's shorting himself."

"Until he has to pay for your lab fees," Brody growled. He picked the spatula back up again and stirred the rice that he'd added, tossing in vegetables every now and then.

Well, maybe that explained some of his attitude. He wasn't being weird about the blood test, not really, but he was being weird about something. If it was Dr. Watson, then she couldn't really blame him. The guy was an ass, and there was no denying that. "Just ignore him. He'll be over it by tomorrow."

"It's not any of my business, but I really don't like the guy. Even before he said anything to you." His stirring became a little more aggressive.

"You'd like him even less if you spent more time in there," she noted cooly, realizing just how many things she could complain about if she truly opened up.

He let out a bit of a laugh, but not a humorous one. "When you came into the shop and said you worked for him, you didn't say anything about all of that."

"He has a lot of patients," she reasoned. "You never know if one of them might be right around the corner and happen to overhear. Plenty of them are loyal enough that they'd gladly run right in there and tell him what I said, and then I'd be out of a job. That's the last thing I need."

"Mm." It was barely a grumble on his part.

Robin was silent for a time as she watched him cook. He obviously knew what he was doing. He added ingredients with little thought, tasting the sauce and grabbing more seasoning off the shelf above the stove. The cutting board and knife on the other side of the kitchen showed her he'd actually prepped everything himself instead of buying it prechopped like most people did these days. He was a man of hidden talents—many, from what she could tell thus far. Something still seemed to be hiding under the surface, a splinter that had yet to work its way out. What was it? Was he married? Had a kid he hadn't told her about?

He plated their meals and carried them to the dining table adjacent to the kitchen before grabbing a beer for himself out of the fridge. His eyes never lifted to hers. "I hope you like it."

"I'm sure I will." It smelled amazing, and everything looked as professional as if they'd gone to a restaurant to dine. There wasn't a thing wrong with this picture, but she felt the tension between them like a hard metal rod that poked her in the chest and kept her from getting any closer.

"It's really good," she said after she'd had a few bites. It'd been so easy to go out for burgers with him on his motorcycle, and even easier to fall into bed together. So why was this all so awkward now?

"Thanks. When I was still interning as a tattoo artist, I didn't make much money. Stir fry can be a great way to use up leftovers, plus I can't seem to help but make a ton of it." He put his fork down and looked at her.

Not just looked at her. Brody studied her. He reached the very depths of her soul, the intensity of his eyes increasing the longer he looked.

"What is it?" She put her fork down.

"I want—no, I need—to tell you something."

Ah, so here it was. He was a con man, or he committed tax fraud, or the mob was after him. Something.

Brody folded his hands on the table in front of him. The tendons in his throat shifted as he clenched his jaw. "I was perfectly honest with you when I told you the blood test would come back negative. I'm in perfect health."

"That's...good." She'd never doubted he was honest about that, so this statement made her even more uneasy.

"What happened today wasn't your fault. It was mine." Brody sighed and swiped a hand through his hair. "I bit you."

Robin pressed her lips together. "Brody, I've been in the dental industry for a long time now. I know what it feels like when someone bites me, and that wasn't it."

"That's because it wasn't the kind of bite you're used to. It wasn't a human one."

What he said was complete nonsense, yet it still made her heart thump louder against her ribs.

His hands were flat on the table on either side of his plate now. "Robin, I'm a wolf shifter. I lost control of myself for a second, and my fangs came down. One of them pierced your fingertip, which means you'll most likely become one, too."

Silence fell like a heavy blanket over her ears. When Brody didn't say anything else, she found a bubble of laughter erupting from her lips. "I appreciate you making me laugh about it. You didn't have to go quite that far, though."

After a minute, when her laughter settled down, Robin realized that Brody wasn't laughing along with her.

"I'm serious," he said quietly. "I know it's hard for you to believe, but it's true."

She knew he was a jokester, but this was taking things a bit too far. "Come on, Brody. You don't really expect me to believe—"

He smiled, showing his fangs.

Robin shot out of her chair. It skidded across the floor behind her and wobbled on its feet, something she could certainly relate to at the moment. "Um, that's one hell of a party trick."

He came around the table toward her, sending a rush of fear through her stomach. But when he spoke again, she could see that the teeth were no longer there. "Robin, I'll give you all the proof you need until you believe me. I didn't want to tell you, at least not yet. It's too soon, no matter what I feel about you. But it's important that you know this."

She put out a hand to keep him at a distance. He respected that, which she was grateful for, but it didn't make it any easier to wrap her head around this. "Brody, I don't know what to say."

"Why don't you sit back down? We'll talk."

"I don't think I can eat right now." Her stomach churned, and food wouldn't make it any better.

"Over here." He guided her toward the couch across from the Eames chair and drawing supplies she'd thought were so charming before. "I need to tell you what to expect."

Her body stiffened as she drew closer to the couch. She didn't want to sit down on the plush fabric, and she didn't want to hear what he had to say. It was all scary. And crazy. It was fucking crazy. "No. This isn't right. I'm going home." She stepped past him toward the door.

"You're going to need help with this, Robin." He caught up to her at the door, touched her elbow, and turned her toward him. Those hazel eyes, the color of the forest floor in fall, held her. "I understand if you're angry with me, but really, this is important. We've got to talk about it."

Robin looked up into that handsome face, the face of an artist, the face of a mature man who knew who he was and had learned not to put up with bull-shit. Or at least, that's what she'd thought it was. He was still handsome, but she no longer knew exactly what she was looking at. "It figures, you know? It figures that I would put myself out there, even though I knew it was too soon, and this is what I'd get on the first try. A fucking wolf man!"

She yanked the door open and didn't bother to close it as she stormed out to her car, fumbling for her key fob. Let him follow her if he wanted to, but he wasn't going to stop her from leaving.

When she fired up the engine, though, she could see that he was still standing in the open doorway. He still looked just as pleading, just as sad. The tears that pricked her eyes were pure anger and frustration. "You're cracking up, Robin," she said to herself, somehow managing to back out of the driveway despite her blurred vision and shaking fingers. "That's it. You're fucking cracking up."

As she sped down the road, hurt began to replace the anger. She'd really thought there might be something there with Brody. How could she have been so wrong?

9

"So, that's about it," Brody concluded. He paced the room, restless and irritated. It'd been just as hard to tell his family as he thought it would be, or at least it was hard to start. Once he did, though, it was like the floodgates had opened. Everything had come gushing out, unstoppable. He only felt a little better now that it was out. "I knew there was something between us, and I admit that I held back a bit because I knew she was human. It made me doubt myself."

"I think that's reasonable," Rex said quietly. He sat next to his mate, Lori, with his hands behind his head.

"Yeah, I guess you'd know. Still, that all worked out just fine for you. Knowing what we know now, it was always going to. But for me? And for Robin? I just don't know." His wolf was just as edgy as it'd been ever since he'd met Robin, but it was a different sort of agitation now. He still wanted to be near her, and before, it'd only been a matter of figuring out how to spend time with her. Now she didn't even want to see him, and that changed the game completely.

"Do we know with absolute certainty that she's going to change?" Rex asked. "Is it possible that there wasn't enough of a transmission?"

Their sister Dawn, who'd collapsed into a recliner after a long shift, lifted her hands in the air and let them fall. "All we really have is anecdotal evidence. It's not the same as human medicine, where specified trials with specific variables have been tested. The safest bet, of course, is to assume that she'll become a shifter."

"Sounds like she wasn't too pleased about that," Max noted.

"It's a hard pill to swallow," Lori replied. "Even if you come to accept it later."

"I've got to figure out how to deal with this whether she accepts it or not." Brody dug his hands into his hair, leaving it even more rumpled than his bike had made it on the swift ride over to the Glenwood packhouse. "She doesn't know how any of this works, and she won't listen to me. She could put herself in danger, not to mention the rest of us. I'm so sorry."

Rex leaned forward and braced his elbows on his knees. "We're going to figure it out, Brody. It's not like you're in this alone."

He eyed his older brother, the one who'd always been the favorite, the one who led their pack. So many times, Brody had resented him for that, but it didn't stop him from seeing that Rex had been literally born for this position. He could've ranted and railed at Brody, chewing him out for being so careless. It wouldn't have done any good, but it would've been an expected reaction from most. Instead, he just promised they'd work together to fix it. And right now, Brody would do anything to make that happen.

"Well, there's not much we can do about it right now." Max stood and clapped Brody on the shoulder. "You need to clear your head. Let's go for a run."

He wanted to say no for the sheer idea of denying himself something, but Brody knew he was right. They went upstairs and out the back door, straight into the woods. A few steps along the pathway and Brody could feel the cool earth under his paws as his back stretched and his muscles tightened. His sharp hearing picked up every twig and pine needle that crunched beneath him, and the dim light of the moon was more than enough to light his way. *Thanks.*

No problem. Max darted out in front of him and led the way, barreling down the trail at full speed and kicking up dirt.

It was just like him, and it made Brody ramp up his speed. He felt the air rushing into his lungs and the blood singing through his veins. Wind infiltrated his thick coat, and he gave barely a thought to the coordination of four legs instead of two as they raced up and down the rocky hillsides.

Eventually, when they were quite a way from the packhouse, Max slowed. *You really like this Robin, don't you?*

It's more than that, Brody admitted.

I had a feeling. Max trotted up onto a ridge line and loped down it, taking in the view.

Brody followed at a short distance. *I didn't think I'd ever feel the same way again. She's made me realize just how much I've been missing.*

Is that what this is? Are you just trying to fill the void that Danielle and Devin left behind?

It felt like an unfair question, but Brody couldn't

blame him. He'd fallen hard before, and there was a hell of a lot on the line. *I wondered, but no. This is more. This hasn't been that slow burn of attraction and comfort. This was instantaneous, overwhelming, and impossible to ignore. I think I might've been able to keep myself under control if it hadn't been for that shitbag boss of hers. He made me feel like I needed to protect her.*

The best of us lose control every now and then. Max headed down off the edge of the ridgeline, easily navigating the steep slope until they rejoined another trail. It was a narrow one, frequented only by the Glenwoods and other animals who happened to come this way. *Now, you just have to decide what you're going to do about it.*

I need to give her some space, some time to process. Then I'm going to try again. I can't just give up on her and wait for her to come to me. As soon as he thought it, the idea solidified in his mind as the clear and obvious choice. Max had been right. Coming out for a run and getting some of the extra lupine energy out of his system was just what he needed. *She might not be pleased to see me at first, but—wait, do you smell blood?*

Yeah. This way. Max picked up speed again, his dark fur flying through the night.

The two wolves darted through the trees as the

sharp, coppery scent grew stronger. They skidded to a halt when they found the source.

Holy shit.

Holy shit is right. The woman's body was curled on its side, and blood trailed from her lips. Brody's eyes zeroed in on the raccoon tattoo on her calf. *She's been in the shop before.*

I don't sense anyone else in their wolf form right now. We'd better get back to the packhouse and call Kane.

In agreement, Brody followed him. The run back felt much longer than the one out had been, the knowledge of the dead woman dragging their footsteps. As they moved along, Brody was trying to figure out just what he'd smelled back there. Blood, yes, but there were other scents as well. People didn't realize just how much they picked up when they were out in the world. Someone who'd been in a coffee shop in the morning would still smell like it in the afternoon. It irritated him that he couldn't sort them all out right now.

Kane was on patrol, and he arrived at the packhouse quickly. He listened to what Max and Brody had to say and gave them a brief nod. "All right. The two of you were out for a hike. The only way you'd be that far out there at night would be if you got lost, so I'd suggest sticking with that. I'll tell the chief, and we'll get onto it."

"This is getting a little disturbing," Rex pointed out. "There was already a woman found in Spencer Butte Park, which is technically part of our territory. This one's even closer to home. I need to know what's happening here."

Kane folded his arms in front of his chest, accentuating his broad shoulders in his uniform. "I get it, and we're working on it. We're a little short on staff at the moment, but I'll let you know any further information as soon as I get it."

"I can get back out there with some of the others," Brody volunteered, not particularly interested in sitting around and waiting. "We can shift and canvass for clues. No offense, but it'll be a lot faster with our noses."

"Hey, nothing's going to keep the wildlife out of the forest," Kane reasoned, giving them his permission as indirectly as he could.

"You sure?" Max asked. "You've already been out there and back, not to mention you've had several training sessions with the younger wolves over the past week."

"You've got other stress, too," Rex pointed out, though he wouldn't say what that stress was when there were others in the room who didn't know about the predicament with Robin just yet. "You don't have to do this."

"I want to," Brody replied instantly. He knew there was no way he could just sit there. The image of that woman haunted him already. She'd been alive and well when he'd seen her just a few hours earlier, and it was disturbing to think that it'd all changed so fast. "I'll go see who's available."

There was no shortage of volunteers once they knew what Brody was up to. He led out a dozen other wolves, charging forward at the head of the pack and refusing to stop until they reached the victim. The numerous scents assaulted his nose once again. He'd managed to clear his head and make a decision when it came to Robin, but he was rattled again and still couldn't sort them all out. Something nagged at the back of his brain, and frustration began to mount.

Spread out, he commanded. *We need to get as much information as possible. If you find anything note-worthy, we need to make sure we know the position well. I don't want to report back to Rex and Kane with nothing.*

He stood for a moment as he watched the other wolves, readily obeying his commands. They moved silently through the woods, collecting information with their eyes, ears, and noses that humans would never notice. Brody just had to hope it'd be enough.

With one last glance toward the victim, who wouldn't be found by the police for some time yet, Brody put his nose to the ground and followed suit. Desperation filled him as he moved methodically in a fan shape, weaving back and forth to avoid missing anything. He *had* to find something. He *had* to figure this out.

He ignored that desperation at first, chalking it up to the shock of finding a body when they'd least expected to. That was the sort of thing that would rattle anyone, and he wasn't immune. But as he searched, Brody knew there was more to it than that.

Two women. Two women had been killed and dumped in the woods, or perhaps killed in the woods. Brody didn't know how she'd died; he only knew that being near the victim made a sinking pit open up in his stomach. This was too close to home and wasn't just a one-off event.

What about Robin? Was she safe from whatever was happening? He had no evidence suggesting she'd be the next victim, but that strange nagging at the back of his mind wouldn't let go. At the very least, he knew she'd be vulnerable due to her state.

There was no telling when she'd shift, and whether she wanted to need him or not, she would.

He pulled in a deep breath and continued his search. Brody had already decided that she needed her space, but it was going to be hard to give it to her.

10

———

"HOW MANY CUPS HAVE YOU HAD TODAY?"

Robin grabbed the half-and-half and added a generous splash to her mug. "Not enough, apparently. I'm exhausted. I didn't get much sleep last night."

"You shouldn't let it stress you out," Maggie said sympathetically. "Dr. Watson is always pissed about something. He's probably already forgotten about it anyway, so try not to let him ruin your day."

Slowly stirring the half-and-half in, Robin watched the white swirl turn a deep caramel until everything in the mug was just the right color. Maggie thought she was still upset over yesterday's incident during Brody's cleaning, both the blood exposure and Brody's confrontation with Dr.

Watson. It had all felt like a big deal at the time, so it made sense that Maggie would think she'd still be upset over it.

The truth, however, was much more complicated.

"I won't," she promised anyway. "I really just need to get through the day. I don't have the energy to argue with anyone. I accidentally flossed my ten o'clock twice. She didn't notice, or if she did, she didn't say anything."

"I'd suggest taking the day off if I didn't think Watson would blow a gasket over it," Maggie said as she turned away to answer the phone. "Watson Dentistry. This is Maggie. How can I help you today? Yes, just a moment." She pressed the hold button and turned back to Robin. "It's your doctor's office."

"Okay. I'll get it in my exam room." Robin knew she had a clear history and had no doubt the results would be fine. The test was more for Brody's sake than her own. But if she was now part-wolf like Brody claimed she might be, would the test somehow pick up on that? Her hand shook as she picked up the handset and pressed the button next to the flashing light. "This is Robin."

"Hey, this is Darcy from Dr. Bennett's office. I just wanted to give you a call and let you know your lab results came in a bit early, and everything is negative."

She closed her eyes and braced her forehead on the wall. "Thank you, Darcy. Um, did you guys happen to see anything else?"

"We didn't. Are you feeling well?"

What could she say? That she was mostly okay, with no fever or anything, but there was a chance she might sprout fur and start howling at the moon at some point? They'd bring her in for an evaluation, and she'd end up in the psych ward. Not that she'd blame them. If Brody hadn't given her the proof she'd practically demanded, she wouldn't believe it either. "Yeah. I'm fine. Just thought I'd check."

"Okay, well, call us if there's anything you need," Darcy reminded her pleasantly. "Have a great day!"

"You, too."

But how could she? The only way Robin was going to get through the day was by diving into her work. If she was busy, at least the day would feel like it was going by a little faster. Robin cringed as she began working with the disinfectant to ready the room for the next patient. It'd always been a sharp, crisp smell, but now it seemed to be stabbing her right in the nose. Her eyes watered, and she glanced at the spray bottle to make sure she was using the right thing. It was all fine, as far as she could tell. It was just her.

With her eyes still stinging, Robin escorted her next patient back a few minutes later and got her settled. "Okay, so no changes to your medical history, and you're not due for x-rays today, so I can save you from that. Has anything been bothering you lately?"

"No." Melissa Steward, a young professional who came in regularly for her cleanings, settled happily into the exam chair. "Everything's great!"

"That's good to hear. How's your day been so far?" She was used to a bit of idle chitchat with her patients, so fortunately, she could do it on autopilot when her brain was fuzzy from lack of sleep.

"Pretty good. I'm in line for a promotion very soon." Melissa gave a self-satisfied smile.

"Good for you." As Robin began her exam, she frowned. The heavy mixture of bergamot and dark vanilla was an odd choice for Melissa. There was another note in there, too. Something a bit spicy and sweet, the sort of thing you'd find in the back of your spice cabinet and hardly ever used. Nutmeg, maybe. "What kind of perfume are you wearing?"

"It's Gucci Flora," Melissa replied when Robin took the mirror from her mouth. "I don't usually like to indulge too much because I'm always saving my money, but I decided to splurge on a little something for myself."

Yes, some of those bright scents were layered in there, but they were thickly covered by the man's cologne that had been transferred to Melissa's skin more recently. Robin had to wonder if there was a certain reason she was in line for that promotion. "It's lovely."

Fortunately, the bits of conversation moved on to other bland things like the weather, making Robin's job a bit easier until the phone rang and jolted her upright. She glared at the phone, wondering why someone would direct a call to her extension when she was with a patient. But the light that indicated an incoming call wasn't lit up. Frowning, Robin got up and stepped to the doorway. Maggie was in the front office, scheduling an appointment on the phone. Everything looked completely normal. She was losing her mind.

"Sorry about that," she said as she opened a cabinet. "Would you like cinnamon, bubblegum, or mint fluoride today?" Not that the smell or taste of any of them sounded appealing at the moment.

"Mint, please."

When Melissa had left, Robin turned to the computer to check her schedule. The newest scheduling software was supposed to be far more efficient, but the tiny font had become nearly impossible to read. She automatically grabbed her reading glasses and perched them on her nose, feeling like an old librarian. She'd never needed contacts or glasses when she was younger, so buying the glasses—or 'cheaters' as her grandmother had called them—had been like a stab in the gut. She hadn't turned gray yet, nor had she experienced all the hot flashes and mood swings that were supposed to go along with getting older, but the glasses let her know it was only a matter of time. The vision was the first thing to go, they always said.

She peered through the glasses and blinked. Was it possible that the font had gotten even smaller overnight with some cruel update? But everything on the screen was blurry, no matter how much she pulled her head back or pushed her face forward. Whipping the glasses off her face to clean them, Robin scowled at the offending computer screen.

But it was entirely clear.

Robin looked down at the glasses in her hand. Yes, these were absolutely the purple tortoiseshell frames she'd picked out. When she lifted her eyes back to the screen, it was still perfectly clear.

She set them aside. Of all the strange things that

seemed to be happening to her lately, this wasn't the hill to die on. Robin would let this one go for now.

But that was hard to do when she stepped out into the hallway and heard the cacophony of the entire office come crashing down on her ears. The high whizzing of a drill. The gargling of a patient, which Robin had long ago learned not to be bothered by, but that now made her want to gag. Both familiar and strange voices. The shrill beeping of the x-ray machine. It was a lot. Too much. How had she never noticed it before?

"You all right?" Maggie was standing behind her desk, leaning on the counter and peering at her curiously. "I can make some more coffee if you'd like."

"No. I mean, no thank you." Robin was starting to wonder if she'd had too many cups as it was. Or perhaps it was the combination of too much caffeine and too little sleep, with a heap of stress piled on top. "I'm just going to take a quick break. Would you mind covering for me?"

"Of course. Your next appointment hasn't even checked in yet, and Watson has one of his specials, so you've got some time."

"Thanks." Robin didn't have the room in her brain nor the energy in her body to even worry about who Watson was with or what he was doing.

She stumbled into the employees-only bathroom and locked the door behind her, the sharp tick of metal on metal making her want to grind her teeth.

Closing the toilet seat lid, she slowly lowered herself down and buried her face in her hands. "Get a grip. You're fine. You're just stressed. People go through shit like this all the time. Okay, maybe not exactly like this. But they get stressed, and it makes them go a little nutty. How many patients have you seen come in for a cleaning who act like they're being walked to the electric chair?"

But all the logic and reason in the world weren't helping. It was one thing to talk herself through exhaustion, but that was the least of her problems. Was she really going to turn into a wolf? And what did that even mean? She couldn't wrap her brain around it, no matter how hard she tried. She simply had no information and no basis to lay it down on.

"That's because it's bullshit," she decided. "Brody played a trick on me. A really good trick, but a trick nevertheless. He's an artist and probably has some oddball friends who do special effects or something. It was a shitty way to dump me, but I guess it worked."

Anger moved in over the worry and tension. What an asshole! Brody had seemed so interested in her, but if something had made him change his mind, he could've been mature enough to just say so. At her age, the men she'd be dating should know how to handle things like that better. How old did she have to get before she found someone who'd actually grown up?

Slapping her hands on her thighs, Robin got up with renewed determination. She wasn't going to let him get to her like this. Brody had taken up a small part of her time, and she'd gotten a great night of sex out of it. That didn't mean he had any sort of control over her. He wasn't even there to see what he was doing to her, so why should she let this bother her at all?

She moved to the sink and flicked on the cold water. Robin had been too drained that morning to bother with makeup, so at least she wouldn't be ruining it. The chilly water felt fantastic on her hands. She gasped as it hit her face, but Robin splashed it on three more times. It was time to wake up, get over whatever she was letting happen to her, and move on.

But as she straightened up and looked in the mirror, her eyes landed on a dark hair that jutted out from her face. "No friggin' way." Robin leaned closer. It was just on the border between her upper lip and her cheek. It wasn't the first time she'd had a random hair pop up somewhere, but this thing was already an inch long.

Some of that fear began to creep in again, but Robin shoved it back down. Okay, so she had an embarrassing hair on her face. That happened to people all the time, or there wouldn't be so many hair removal products on the market. She turned to the small set of lockers behind her; one was labeled for each staff member so they could keep a few things there. Sifting past a box of granola bars and a zippered bag of tampons, she grabbed a little makeup bag and fished out a pair of tweezers. Quick and easy solution.

Turning back to the mirror, Robin stretched the skin around the hair tight. She clamped the tweezers down hard and gave them a good yank.

It almost sent her reeling to the floor as pain radiated through her face. A string of every expletive spilled from her mouth as she waited for the pain to go away. Tears blurred her eyes, the same kind that would've come if she'd yanked out a nose hair. What the hell was happening?

Leaning against the wall, Robin looked down at the tweezers still clutched in her hand. She'd managed to remove the hair, at least. It was thick and dark, and much longer than anything else she'd ever seen on her face. It was different than any hair she'd found anywhere else, for that matter. As much as she didn't want it to be, Robin knew what it was. This wasn't simply a sign of her getting older, and it didn't mean she should book an appointment for a very thorough wax.

It was a wolf whisker.

Robin sank down the wall. Regret moved through her as she remembered how Brody had tried to keep her at his place. She could still see the pain and worry in his eyes—the pure sadness, even. He'd said they needed to talk, that there were things she should know, that she'd need help. She'd been too scared and hurt and confused to bother listening to him at the moment.

He was a wolf. She'd seen his teeth, and apparently, she'd already had one of them pierce her finger. It was just as real as it was terrifying. Robin swallowed. She wanted to be angry at him because it was the easiest thing to do, but she was frightened more than anything. Frightened for herself. Frightened of him.

Staring at that whisker in her hand, though, she knew what she needed to do.

Brody was the only person she could turn to.

11

THE DAY HAD DRAGGED ON, AND ROBIN WAS MORE than happy when it was time for her to go home. She was going to take a long, hot bath and then fall into bed with meditation music on. The emotional roller coaster she'd been on since the night before had gotten to be far too much to handle, and she was done with it.

But when she was finally at home alone, she found that sitting still in a tub of water was the last thing she wanted to do. Everything smelled intensely strong. Even the giant bottle of lavender bubble bath she'd bought at Costco and had used a million times was far too perfumy. Ignoring that, she felt a restlessness inside that wouldn't let her sit back and relax. With the tub drained and clean sweats on, she couldn't do anything but pace through the house, pretending to tidy up.

Her mind was busy, too. She could call Brody or go by his house. She could even stop in at his shop, but that would be too dramatic. Then again, did she have to get a hold of him right away. Maybe she should give herself some time to think, then sleep, and then think it all over again when she was feeling more rational. There was no point in rushing things, after all.

The ding from her phone had her pulling it out of her pocket. It was a text from Brody.

I'd like to stop by if that's okay.

Her breath rushed out in a sigh, and she closed her eyes. He was taking care of at least part of the decision for her. Robin's nerves jangled as she texted back a simple *okay*. She needed this, whether she wanted it or not.

She felt him before she heard him, a strange agitation in her chest that made her snap her head up from the pile of laundry she was folding. She padded to the back door and stepped out onto the deck.

Brody stood there, just below the short flight of steps that led down into the yard. His eyes looked just as hollow as hers felt. "Do you always walk out into the darkness to meet strange guys on your back porch?"

"Well, the light—" Robin had turned around to gesture at the deck light, but she hadn't turned it on at all. She hadn't even needed it. "I guess that just depends on whether or not the guy has actually turned me into a wolf."

He took a careful step up onto the first stair. "Robin, I know you need some time to process this. It's a big deal and can't be easy for you. I was going to stay away for a while until you were ready to talk, but I'm concerned."

She wrapped her arms around herself, though she wasn't cold. "Why?" Was something going to happen to her? Something worse than turning into a wild beast?

Brody inched up another step. "Another woman was found dead in the woods last night. I don't know what's happening, but I want to know that you'll be able to protect yourself if you need to."

She squinted at him, but she could see him with perfect clarity. He still had that same pitiful look in his eyes that she'd seen when she'd left his house. There was concern there, too. The hateful thoughts she'd had about him before, when she'd decided that he'd made all of this up just to get rid of her, suddenly made her feel horribly guilty. "I keep my doors locked, and I've got pepper spray."

"No." He ducked his head and let out a little laugh. "I mean, that's great and all. But you have an even better weapon inside you now. Most people aren't going to mess with a wolf, but you'd have to be able to shift into one before you could use it."

"Brody, I don't understand. I'm not entirely sure I've convinced myself that this is real, and I keep waiting to wake up. But my sense of smell is going berserk, and my hearing is super sensitive. I think I even had a whisker sticking out of my face today. Is this just going to happen to me whenever and wherever? Is it something I can control? Is it permanent?" She moved across the deck toward him, realizing she wanted the comfort of someone who knew what was happening. Perhaps the comfort of Brody himself.

"I don't know where you are in your transition, so it's hard to say. Why don't we go find out?" He tipped his head toward the woods behind her bungalow.

She glanced at the darkness behind him. "Are you saying you want me to..." Robin trailed off, not wanting to finish that sentence.

"Yeah. I think it's important. And I'll tell you

everything I can." Brody stepped aside, inviting her out into the shadows.

The fear and uncertainty she'd been suffering with all day had dissipated as soon as he'd arrived, and Robin decided to trust that as she walked with him down into the grass. "I've got a lot of questions."

"I know, and I think I know what the first one is. From what you just told me, I'd say your wolf is already trying to make its first appearance. Can you feel it inside you? It's something that's separate from your human side, yet the two are wholly integrated. It doesn't always agree with you, either." He smiled a little as he said that.

There was that charm she'd fallen for, both boyish and beguiling. "I might. I can't seem to sit down, even though I'm exhausted."

He nodded. "With practice, you'll be able to control it. You'll also be able to control when and where you shift, but again, that's with practice. You can't just do this once and expect to have it down. Even those of us who are born with it need training."

"Us?" Somehow, she'd only been concerned about herself and hadn't realized there would be more than just the two of them. "There are others?"

"Plenty of them," he said with a warm smile as they crossed into the darkest part of the yard. "Now, I want you to take a deep breath. When you let it out, imagine that it's pulling the inside of you out with it, like you're turning yourself inside out. Let go of everything you associate with being human, your grocery list, your job, right down to your fingers and toes."

She filled her lungs and closed her eyes, visualizing herself melting away. But nothing happened.

"That's okay," he encouraged softly before she had the chance to ask what she'd done wrong. "Just try again."

She wouldn't give up on this. She wouldn't let herself. Robin knew she had to do this, or she really would go crazy. The proof that it was all real, the kind of proof that she could see in the mirror, was what she needed. On her next breath, she felt something lurch inside her. A prickling tingle erupted all over her skin, followed by tufts of thick fur that slowly pushed up.

"That's it." Brody was right at her side, talking in that quiet way of his. "Bring it all out. It wants to come out, and all you have to do is let down your defenses so that it can. More deep breaths, Robin."

Her fingers curled, and she watched her nails thicken into claws. Her lower back twinged, worse than the time she'd pulled a muscle lifting a laundry basket. She tried to breathe, but the air was shaky through her throat.

"Surrender yourself to it, Robin. I know it hurts. I promise it gets easier. Just trust me."

And she did. He was the only one she could trust right now, but she wholeheartedly did. Robin twisted her head from side to side as bones crunched, the snapping echoing in her skull. It was a horrid sound, but it brought with it all the things she expected to see. Her muzzle stretched out long and gray at the front of her face. Her arms and legs changed, her knees making more popping noises until everything was oriented the right way. The grass was cool under her feet—not feet, paws. Pain radiated through her, throbbing in her bones, but it was happening.

Once she'd completed her transformation, Brody joined her in his wolf form. *There you go. You did it.*

Holy shit. Robin looked down at herself and wished she had a mirror. Even without one, she could see the beautiful sheen of silver fur. *I'm gorgeous!*

He chuckled. *Yes, you are. Now you should try to take a few steps.*

Though her wolf muscles felt strong, and she was operating on four legs instead of two, Robin hadn't quite gained her balance. She took a step and then stumbled, falling right into his flank.

You're like a really big puppy right now.

She heard the humor in his voice. *Easy for you to say, I guess.* Robin twitched her claws in the grass, trying to stabilize herself as she studied him. He was quite the specimen as a man, but she couldn't deny his beauty as a wolf. His fur was about the same shade as hers, with lighter and darker bits mottled in. She'd never been this close to a wolf before, not even at the zoo. *Damn, he's even more gorgeous than I am.*

Thank you.

Embarrassment felt different in this form. Instead of burning cheeks, she felt her tail try to tuck between her legs. She marveled at even having a tail, but she didn't understand. *I didn't say that out loud, did I?*

Brody turned to face her, a hint of that deep hazel still lingering in his eyes. *Think about it, Robin. You haven't said anything out loud. It's all in your mind. We communicate telepathically.*

No.

Try me, he challenged. *Think about what you had for lunch today.*

That was easy enough. She'd packed a tuna salad

sandwich with whole wheat bread and a small container of baby carrots. Her stomach hadn't particularly wanted it at the moment, but she'd forced it down because she'd known she needed any energy she could get.

I'm not much of a fan of tuna salad, myself.

Robin took a step back. *You can just hear anything I'm thinking?*

Not exactly. You'll be able to refine that as time goes on, only sharing the thoughts you want to.

But why? she insisted, wanting to truly understand this instead of just accepting it. *Why can we do this at all?*

He cocked his head a little. *Basically, you're an honorary member of my pack.* He turned and began walking out into the night.

Robin followed, tripping over herself every few steps as she tried to figure out how to coordinate four legs. Dogs and cats made it look so damn easy, and she resented them at the moment. The claws on her back paws scraped against the backs of her front legs, and her front and hind ends weren't in agreement as to exactly where and how they should be moving. *Pack?*

Sort of like a big, extended family. We take care of each other, in good times and in bad. We're led by an Alpha, someone who's sort of like a father figure for everyone else, regardless of age. In our pack, that happens to be my brother.

Robin tripped again and fell forward, her chin crashing like a downed airplane into the grass. *I don't think I can walk and talk yet.*

That's all right. You'll get a better chance to get your wolf legs as we start sparring.

Sparring? Robin clambered to her feet, sure that she hadn't heard him correctly. *You want to fight me?*

We have to, so you know how to use that new body of yours. Like I said, I want to make sure you're safe. But we're just going to start with a few different moves. Get all your feet under you.

She let out a huff. *They are, thank you very much.*

Brody put his broad side toward her. *Good. Tuck your head down, a little to the side. Run at me, and ram me with your shoulder.*

What?

Aim for right about here. He pressed his muzzle near her flank.

Robin jerked away. *That tickles!*

It won't tickle me if you do it right.

She didn't yet know how to read his eyes, but she didn't miss the innuendo. *I guess we'll just have to find out.*

Once again, Brody set himself up with his broad side toward her. Robin had no idea how much good this was actually going to do, but she'd already come this far. Hoping she could keep her feet moving correctly, she put her head down and barreled toward him. Her shoulder slammed into the side of his body. Brody barely moved, and she went bouncing to the ground.

You could've at least made me feel like I was doing it right. She picked herself up, wondering just how she would get the dirt out of her fur later or if she was even supposed to worry about that.

Brody turned to her. *You did. You're just not strong enough yet. If you can get one of those in on someone who doesn't expect it, you can knock their back legs out from under them. You just have to be ready for the retaliation that's going to come next.*

Which would be? she challenged.

Put your jaws around my throat.

Robin took two steps away, pleased that she'd managed to go backward without falling, but appalled at the idea. *What? I can't do that.*

You can, and you should. The underbelly is the most sensitive place you can go for, but it's hard to get your opponent to expose it if they know what they're doing. If someone comes after your throat, you need to know what it's like. So do it.

Gingerly, feeling like a complete fool, Robin opened her mouth. Brody had lifted his head to give her some space, offering a chance that no one else would if they were actually trying to survive. It didn't help much. She tried one angle and then another, but it was awkward, to say the least.

Kind of like this. Without warning, Brody's teeth flashed. He bowled her over with his shoulder, but his legs braced against her to keep her fall to the ground as a gentle roll. She landed squarely on her back with Brody's jaws wrapped around her throat, just the way he'd tried to tell her.

Robin's breath was ragged, and even in a different form, she couldn't help but remember how things had been with him before. He could snap his teeth shut and kill her in an instant, but it was both that possibility and the knowledge that he wouldn't do it that made a shudder of excitement rise up in her stomach. *Oh. Well. Why didn't you say so?*

He hovered over her, his eyes burning into hers, for a long moment. When he finally stepped over to allow her up, Robin felt how badly she wanted him back. Not just to have things back the way they were between them, but to have him close like that. She didn't care if he was a wolf, a human, or a blue whale. She just wanted him close.

Are you ready for the next one?

The shake that took over her body when she got up was a natural one, and one she hadn't expected. Dirt flew off her fur, solving that problem. *As ready as I'll ever be.*

On second thought, you probably need to know how to defend yourself in that position. With a quick leap, he was on top of her again.

Robin wanted to laugh, and she batted a paw against his muzzle. *Fresh.*

I'll show you fresh.

They rolled and wrestled, tumbling over each other, playing and fighting, darting in and defending. Brody coached her as they went, encouraging her every time she missed and praising her when she didn't. It was far more fun than Robin ever would've realized. The anxiety that'd swept over her over the last twenty-four hours was gone. It wasn't just because she was so thoroughly distracted. It was something else that tugged at her, pulling from the very depths of her soul and reaching out toward Brody. He was her anchor in this unfamiliar storm. This magnetism between them was something she couldn't help, but she didn't want to. She'd never felt anything like this.

Okay, okay! I surrender! He'd been chasing her around the clearing they'd entered, trying to show her all the ways that another wolf could dive in and find her vulnerable spots, but she'd finally lost all of her breath. *I'm pooped!*

Fair enough. Brody trotted to a stop beside her. *I think we've made good progress, anyway. Why don't you just sit down for a bit.*

With more confidence than she'd felt when they'd first come out there, she managed to curl her tail and back legs underneath her and keep her front legs straight. She felt more balanced this way, and she breathed a sigh of relief.

Now, look up. See the moon?

I'm not supposed to howl at it or anything, am I? Because if I am, then I'm not so sure I'm going to be a good wolf.

He sat next to her, lifting his chin. *You can if you want. I don't think she'd mind. Selene's up there, the goddess of the moon. Our pack is devoted to her, but don't start thinking about werewolf movies and the full moon. It's not like that, but that's where some of those old tales came from.*

Robin studied the burning disc in the sky. She'd

been through plenty of science classes, and she knew that the hunk of rock was held in place by Earth's gravitational pull. She knew that it only glowed as it did because of the light it borrowed from the sun. Even so, she could feel its pull on her, one that filled her chest and heart with light. *It's beautiful.*

I think so.

When she finally looked over at him, she saw that Brody was looking straight at her instead of the moon. *Brody, I owe you an apology. I'm sorry I blew up at you. You were trying to do the right thing by telling me about the bite and what would happen because of it. I appreciate it because I think if I hadn't known, it would've driven me even crazier than it already did. Still, I wish I'd been able to calm down and listen to you.*

He turned his gaze back toward the sky, but he leaned so that their shoulders brushed. *That's all right. I knew it wasn't going to be easy, not for either one of us, really. I wasn't ever mad at you for leaving. Just worried.*

Robin thought about that for a moment. *I'm glad you did because I think I needed someone to worry about me. I was so freaked out, not just at your place but even today at work. I didn't know what to think or what I was going to do.*

And now?

Now? Robin gazed up at the sky. Everything felt different as an animal. The sharpened senses she'd experienced during the day had grown even more intense, but they were easier to handle now. Her muscles and brain had no idea how to control this body when she'd first managed to shift into it, but now she felt the power and elegance that came with it. There was still plenty of this journey left, and she wouldn't delude herself into thinking otherwise, but it was a hell of a start. *It's going to take me a while to adjust to this new identity, but I'm kind of grateful for it.*

Hope shimmered in his eyes. *Really? You don't mind it?*

No. Her answer was quick, but it was honest. *It's actually kind of nice to know there's a wolf lurking inside me if I ever need it.*

Never a bad thing to be carrying around, he agreed. *Robin, I know things have been strange lately, but I'd like to take you out again. In human form.*

They were 'out' right now, technically, but she knew that wasn't what he meant. Robin liked the idea either way. *Yeah. That would be great.*

12

"I JUST KNEW I HAD TO GET THIS COMPASS TATTOOED on my foot. I mean, I love to travel. Don't you?"

"Mm." With a paper towel, he wiped off the black ink that'd pooled on her skin and started shading in the arms of the compass. The lines had come out nice and crisp, just as he'd planned. After this bit of shading, he just had to add the splash of color she wanted in the background.

He was in the zone, so he could perform his work without using his whole mind. The rest of it was completely occupied by thoughts of Robin. The night they'd spent together after going out for burgers had been incredible, but their time together as wolves the night before had been downright magical. He hadn't expected their pull to increase that much once they were on four legs, which only proved that his theory about her was right. There was a lot he had yet to tell her. If she'd come around to the idea of being a shifter, maybe the rest wouldn't be so bad.

"Beaches are my absolute favorite," his client continued, gesturing quickly with her hands and making her whole body jerk.

It was a small enough movement in everyday life, but it was enough that it could seriously fuck up a tattoo for an artist that wasn't ready. Brody automatically lifted his needle until she settled back in again, scrunching his brow and hoping she'd get the hint.

"You know, the sun, the sand. Laying out in my favorite little string bikini. Or maybe no bikini at all, depending on where I am," she giggled.

Red and orange on one side, fading across to green and blue. It'd be a good effect when it was all done.

He'd never seen a wolf as stunning as Robin. She may have been a little gawky and uncertain at first, but it'd been endearing to watch her trip all over herself. She put her life and trust in his hands as they worked together. Brody had felt that connection deepen the longer they were out there, and he hadn't wanted it to end.

"I admit, I tend to get a little wild when I'm on vacation. I'd be so embarrassed if someone took my phone and looked through all those crazy pics!" She waggled her phone in the air for emphasis. "But you know, I get a few margaritas in me, and I just can't help myself!"

Robin had done well for someone who'd been human her entire life. Brody could only hope he'd shown her enough so she could keep herself safe if anything happened.

"All right. All I have to do is clean it off, and then you're done."

"Oh, can I take a video? I love this part. So satisfying!" She was already sitting up and aiming her camera.

"Sure." He cleaned it carefully, checking for anything that he'd missed. It was a habit he'd started a long time ago after he'd missed a line when he was just an apprentice. It was a mistake he'd been determined not to make twice, and so far, he'd stuck to that. Everything looked great.

"I'd like to get a photo for my portfolio and records, if you don't mind," he said mildly, knowing she wouldn't. She was obviously more than happy to be on camera.

"Not at all! And if you want to share it on social media or anything, that'd be great!"

"Good deal." When he'd taken off his gloves, he grabbed his phone and snapped a few photos. "Are you happy with it?"

"Are you kidding me?" she gushed. "It's amazing! But I knew it would be. You came highly recommended. For your talent, but also because all my friends said you were hot." She giggled again.

With a new pair of gloves, Brody carefully covered the tattoo in a special jelly and then plastic wrap to keep it safe. "I've got some aftercare sheets for you, but you can always call the shop if you have any concerns or questions. You can pay up front, and you're all done."

"Thank you so much! I just love it!" She batted her eyelashes at him.

It was only then that Brody realized what was actually happening. She'd been flirting with him the whole time. At one point, when he was much younger, he'd liked that idea. More recently, it hadn't mattered much. Now that Robin was in his life, it didn't matter at all. "Thanks. Have a good one."

She was happy with her tattoo, if not with his reaction to her, but he had to count that as a satisfied customer. Brody took a moment to upload the best photo of her tat to a folder in his cloud where he kept all of the work he did, and he tagged it with the date and a few categories so he'd be able to find it later.

As he did, it occurred to him that the media hadn't released the name of the woman with the raccoon tattoo. Brody found it easily enough with a quick search. Then he popped into the shop's files, a different system that tracked names, contact info, and waivers. Sienna Barry. That was her. He hadn't been able to come up with her name off the top of his head, but once all the pieces were there, they fit together perfectly.

He glanced down at her date of birth. Damn. The poor girl was only twenty-five. She had her whole life ahead of her, but now it'd all been taken away. And for what? Why would anyone do such a thing?

Brody put the files and his phone away as he began wiping down the room. The paper towels, gloves, and cups of ink went into the trash. The needles went in the sharps container. He arranged his other equipment so it could be autoclaved. Brody remembered when he was twenty-five. He and Danielle had been together for about five months, long enough for him to get just as excited for her child coming into the world as she was. He'd gone with her to buy all the baby furniture and clothing, and they had diapers and bottles ready to go. Seeing Devin come into the world had been the most exhilarating thing he'd ever experienced. The world had changed for him, making Brody feel like he could do anything. That was when he'd truly knuckled down and gotten serious about tattooing, determined to make good money and a good life for the three of them.

Danielle hadn't been his mate. He'd known it then just as much as he knew it now, but he'd ignored it. Devin hadn't been his son, either. But it was a beautiful start to a perfect little family, and he'd been sure he could make it work.

Some things just weren't possible.

"Hey."

Poppy's knock on the doorway had him looking over his shoulder at her. "Hey."

"That cute girl you just finished with wouldn't shut up about you. I heard her out there while she was paying." Poppy had a sketchbook in her hand and a teasing grin on her face.

"Well, I'm not interested."

"Why not? Ooh, are you actually seeing some-one?" she asked in a singsong voice. "I don't think you've gone out on a date since I started working here."

"I have," he snapped. "I just don't blast it on social media for everyone to see."

"Right. Okay. Forget I asked." She was still smiling. "I just wanted to see what you thought of this." Poppy handed him her latest design.

Brody studied the fine linework that created a smooth, pudgy child's hand clasped around the pinkie of a much older, careworn hand. A father and his child, with smudges of a sunset in the background. "It's great."

"You think the angle is okay? I don't want the hands to look weird."

"No." Brody held it a while longer, studying not only the drawing but the relationship it represented. It was something he'd longed for, something he'd thought he had for a while. He still wanted it, but he didn't know if there'd ever be a chance for it. He was meant to be with Robin. He knew that, and he accepted it readily. But she was already forty and recently divorced. Surely, if she'd wanted kids, she would've had them by now. Was there any chance of them becoming a family?

"No, I think it's awesome," he assured Poppy as

he handed it back to her. "That's going to be one hell of a meaningful piece for someone."

She smiled as she took it back. "Yeah, I think so, too. Thanks." She started to head back toward her own booth.

"Why would you ask me about your design? You're a great artist."

Poppy turned in the doorway and smiled. "Because you're good at what you do, Brody. You think you just sit in here and do your work, but you're more of a leader than you know."

He didn't quite know how to answer that, so he said nothing else and let her get back to her work. When the shop closed and Brody went home to his empty house, he stepped out into the backyard. The high fence meant no one could see him there, so he let his other form take over. Brody lifted his eyes to the moon, a full orb overhead. He prayed to Selene, hoping she could hear and understand his heart. He had to trust that she wouldn't lead him wrong.

13

"That's perfect. It smells fantastic."

The girl working the booth grinned. "All the butterflies think so, too. They're all over the place with this dill we've been growing, and we've actually started an extra patch of it just for them."

"Then I'll take two bundles and some of the basil, too." Brody turned and wagged his eyebrows at Robin. "I hope you like pesto."

"It's one of my favorites," she admitted, deciding he could probably whip up quite the batch, given his talent with stir fry. As Brody finished his transaction, she watched him carefully. He was just a man, at least to the naked eye. No one who saw him exploring the Whiteaker Community Market would have the slightest idea that he was a wolf. That *they* were wolves.

But she knew, and now she had to wonder if that affected how she felt about him. She'd been furious and terrified when he'd told her the news about her new life, but now that she'd gotten past some of that, she found herself wanting to spend more and more time with him. That was why they were walking around The Whit that day, and she doubted it'd be the last time they saw each other.

Did she feel this way because there was something genuine between them, or because he was the only one she could turn to? How could she possibly know?

"See anything you're interested in?" Brody asked as they walked down the row of booths.

"It's hard to say. Everything looks amazing," she admitted. They were surrounded by booths that sold vegetables, herbs, jewelry, and art. The delicious smell of local food simmered through the air, reminding her of all the places they could eat when they were done.

Brody dropped a bill in the open guitar case of a young woman singing her own folksy remixes of popular songs. "I get it. This is one of my favorite things to do on the weekends. It's a feast for the senses."

"Yeah, and I'm starting to get overly stuffed." Colors were brighter and lines were sharper. Everything felt like it was in high definition, and she caught so many snippets of conversations, she could hardly keep track of them.

He slipped his hand into hers, his thick fingers folding in between her own. "You doing okay with it all?"

He didn't have to tell her exactly what he meant. She knew, and it was pretty much the only thing on her mind. There was a remarkable amount of comfort in the way their hands fit together, and she leaned her head against his arm. "I guess I have to say yes, overall."

"But?"

Robin rubbed her lips together. She didn't want to complain. She knew that Brody had done this accidentally, and she saw the worry and guilt in his eyes when they spoke of it.

"I can't help you if you don't tell me," he prodded.

"It's hard to concentrate on my work," she admitted. "I've been worried I'll do something stupid, something I can't control, and then everyone will find out."

"Ah." The way he nodded his head let her know he truly understood. She didn't want to shift while she was at work. "You have to trust yourself. I know that's not easy, especially right now when you feel like you don't have any control. But you know what it felt like before?"

How could she forget the shock to her system when she'd become all the proof she'd needed and transformed into a wolf right in her own backyard? "Definitely."

"Trust me, you'll remember that feeling if it starts to happen on its own. The first shifts come on fairly slowly. It's only once you really know what you're doing that it happens fast, so you should have time to get yourself under control. Granted, I guess I'm not a good person to talk to you about control." Brody grinned, showing his teeth. They were normal human teeth right now, but it was one of his wolf fangs that'd started all of this in the first place.

"I'll keep that in mind." Robin couldn't help but smile at him. He was just so pleasant to be around, creating a deep sense of satisfaction within her even when they were just walking around at a farmers' market. She paused to examine the tiny needle-felted creatures a woman had made by hand. "I guess I'm also a little frustrated because I can't tell my family. We're pretty close. I see them all at least once a week, and my sister is like my best friend. It's a little weird to keep things from them."

"I'm sorry."

She heard the gravity in his voice and looked up quickly.

He tightened his grip on her hand and ducked out of the booth, away from anyone who might over-hear. "I've had to keep this secret from the world for the last forty-two years, but not from my family. I can't imagine how hard that is."

"I'll get used to it, I guess. Hey, do you want to go get something to eat? I'm starving."

Brody gave her an uncertain look. "You don't have to skirt around it just to spare my feelings, Robin. I can't go back and change what I've done. We both know that. But at least let me be here for you while you work through it all. I want to do everything I can for you."

"It really will be okay," she insisted. It was tough not to slip up about it when she talked to Renee, who always wanted a progress report on what was happening between her and Brody. Robin could only give her vague details about the time they spent

together, but not why or how. Still, that wasn't really
his problem, and she wasn't sure she wanted to put
every aspect of her life into his hands just yet. "It's
just going to take me some time. I really am hungry,
though."

Brody didn't look like he quite believed her, but
he let it go. "I was thinking about going over to
Better Living Room, if you're up for a bit more
walking."

"Sure." In fact, she was more up for walking than
she remembered being in a long time. Moving her
body felt good, and she was starting to enjoy the way
her muscles moved and stretched inside of her. If it
was always like this as a shifter, she could understand why Brody was so fit.

The brewery and restaurant was aptly named.
The teal and orange color scheme gave a cozy feel
that contrasted with the industrial attitude of stain-
less steel and metalwork. Eclectic mixes of furniture
created homey settings for friends to gather, and
comfortable chairs huddled around tables for a
welcoming dining experience. They grabbed a table
on the patio.

Automatically, Robin pulled out her reading
glasses when she picked up the menu. The whole
thing was nothing but a blur, and she whipped them

off again. "Apparently, I've got to start remembering that I don't need these anymore. I keep bringing them everywhere I go, but they're hindering me more than helping me."

Brody plucked them out of her hand and tucked them in the pocket of his flannel shirt, which he wore over a fitted white tee. "I can't deny there are downsides to our situation, but never having to go to the optometrist or dentist isn't one of them."

"Depriving all these specialists of their copays," she returned, glad the mood had lifted a little. She wanted to enjoy her time with Brody instead of stewing about her complaints.

She chose a Bourbon Renewal off the menu, something she'd had before but never quite like this. The lemon and black currant flavors came through for her more than they had before. Eventually, she'd get used to noticing every little thing. For the moment, she was determined to enjoy it.

Two tiny hands suddenly clutched her leg, and Robin looked down to find herself looking into a big pair of brown eyes. "Well, hello there."

"Hi!" The little boy grinned.

"Cole! Come back over here! I'm so sorry!" The boy's mother came running over from their table to fetch him. "He's a little too friendly."

Robin smiled at her, and she found she was almost sorry to see little Cole go. "It's not a problem at all. He's adorable."

When she looked back up, Brody was watching her over the top of his can as he took a sip of his Gin Rickey. He gestured toward the table where Cole had returned to his parents and two siblings. "Did you ever think about having kids?"

The swelling that the little boy had created in her heart emptied like a popped balloon. "Yeah. I really wanted to, and I'd hoped to start a family a long time ago. When my ex and I first got married, I decided to wait a couple of years to make sure we were financially stable. It's probably a good thing I did because it was during that time that I realized JC himself wasn't stable in any way."

Brody's elbows were on the table now, and he leaned forward. "So then you just never did?"

She lifted a shoulder. "It didn't seem fair to bring a child into something like that." There were times when she'd regretted that situation, wondering if having a loving mother who tried her hardest would be enough. JC was difficult enough for her to deal with, though, and she had to be glad that she hadn't forced someone else to do so. "What about you?"

"I never had any of my own." He took another sip

and then looked down at his can for so long that Robin wasn't sure if he would continue. "When I was in my twenties, I started dating this girl named Danielle. She was pregnant, and the father didn't want to have anything to do with it. I pretty much stepped right in. I was there when Devin was born, when he took his first steps, and when he went to kindergarten for the first time."

As he spoke, Robin realized how much easier it was to see Brody—a man she'd only known for a short time—in that position than it'd ever been to see JC like that. "That was sweet of you."

"I've wondered about that, actually." He glanced over at Cole's family again. "When he was about six years old, Danielle decided she wanted to move on. Things had been falling apart between us for quite some time, so I could deal with that. But that meant that Devin and I weren't in each other's lives anymore. I got to give him one last hug, and that was it. I never got to see him again."

"Brody," she whispered. Robin reached across the table and stroked her fingertip down the back of his hand. "I'm so sorry."

He shook his head. "It was just one of those things. It felt right at the time, but later, I had to wonder if I'd done him a disservice. Poor kid had a father figure, but then all of a sudden, he didn't. I tried to get her to let me see him a couple of times a month, and I even offered to help take care of some of his expenses, but Danielle didn't want to get tangled up in that sort of thing if she was going to find a new man."

"She was thinking about herself instead of her son," Robin concluded, knowing that JC would've been the exact same way. He wouldn't have wanted to let himself be held back by children when he could've been exploring something he wanted to pursue. He always thought he was moving on to something bigger and better with one scheme or another, but all he actually did was waste time and money.

Robin had definitely made the right decision by not having a family with him, but she'd also made the wrong decision by being with him in the first place.

Their conversation moved on to careers, family, and their first cars as teenagers. The bourbon cocktail went beautifully with her fried fish sandwich. Robin questioned herself when she let the waiter get her a second one, but she was having too much fun to stop now. Brody was easy to be around. That was one of the things she liked about him the most, although it certainly didn't hurt that he was hot. He wasn't a guy who needed his ego boosted to feel important, nor was he trying too hard to impress her. He was a real person, someone she would've only been able to dream of up until now.

She knew her smile was a little too big as she polished off her sandwich and wiped her fingers. "You know, there's something about you that I just can't resist."

The corner of his mouth turned up as he pointed to her cocktail. "I'm going to point out that you've had two of those before you say something you might regret."

"I mean it, whether I've been drinking or not. I think I started feeling it right when I first met you. I was horrified when Poppy said she couldn't do my tattoo, and I wasn't comfortable with some random guy doing it. But you were different."

"As I recall, you were pretty hesitant," he noted as he dipped a fry in ketchup.

"At first, yes, but that was just because a lot of other emotions were swirling around." She gestured wildly toward the side of her head as though that would help it all make sense. "You made me feel so relaxed. I couldn't stop thinking about you after I left, and not just because you did a good job on my tattoo."

"So it wasn't too much that I made an unnecessary dental appointment?" Brody asked, one eyebrow quirking up.

"It stopped me from having to make an unnecessary tattoo appointment," she replied with a laugh. "No, it was actually really nice to know you wanted to see me again."

"I'm glad to hear it." Brody reached across the table and took her hand in his.

Robin wove her fingers between his and felt that swell inside her like the tide, pulling her closer to Brody. She wanted to come around the table and curl up against his chest. "I wish I knew how to explain it. Even when we're together, I can't get close enough to you. Right now, I'm kind of pissed at this table for being between us. And when we're not together, I just want to walk out the door and go find you. I know that sounds crazy, but it's true." She'd felt it so many times already, and she could feel it even more right now.

"It's not crazy." His thumb rubbed slowly over the back of her hand. He glanced to the side, where Cole and his family had been sitting, but they were gone. They were the only ones in their little part of the patio right now. "I feel the exact same way about you. Every fiber of my being reaches for you. My wolf goes crazy when you're not around, and then it goes crazy in a completely different way when you are."

Robin's cheeks felt warm. She knew that was probably from the bourbon, but the warmth flooding through the rest of her wasn't. Earlier that afternoon, she'd had doubts about why she felt so strongly for Brody, but now she understood there was no reason to question it. Yes, she was relying on him to help her with her wolf, but this had come over her before that wolf was even inside her. She could feel it now. It was subtle, but it fit the description Brody had given her of how it felt to have this other being living within her. It reached out toward Brody's beast, longing for more than just their hands to touch. "I think I'm starting to understand the feeling."

He licked his lips and took her hand in both of his now. "Robin, there's something I haven't told you yet about being a shifter."

She tipped her head, slightly disturbed by what felt like a sudden change in subject. Robin was content to revel in their feelings for each other, and the logistics of changing from human to wolf and back again could wait for another time. "It's all right. I know there's a lot, and we can't get it all in at once. We could have another, um, training session if you'd like." Robin was drunk, all right, but it didn't have anything to do with the alcohol. She was drunk on Brody and on what they'd managed to find between them.

"I don't think this can wait any longer." Brody leaned forward, those remarkable hazel eyes of his intense on hers. "Robin, there are a lot of things about shifters that are different from the way humans are. You know that already, but it's not just about changing shape or having excellent hearing. It's also about the things we believe and feel."

A jolt of nerves bolted through her. He was so passionate right now that it made her wonder exactly where he was going with all of this.

"We believe that there is only one true soulmate out there for each of us. Those two people are fated to each other, drawn together like forces of nature. I know that it's quick for me to say something that sounds like such a big commitment, but that's why you feel that pull toward me, Robin. We're destined to be together. We're mates."

The jolt of nerves zipped down to her stomach. "If that's true, and if that's how you know, then how could each of us have been with other people before?"

He made a helpless gesture with his hand. "It happens. For me, I knew Danielle wasn't my true mate. I was ready to settle down, but I hadn't met you yet. I'm sure, in some ways, it was no different for you. People get married and then divorced all the time, and I like to think they then have a chance to find the person they're supposed to be with."

While some of that was all very reasonable, there was another aspect that Robin was having trouble understanding. "But I was just a boring old human until a week ago. How could you have been fated to someone who doesn't exist? I mean, in the sense that if I wasn't a shifter, I couldn't have been fated to you."

Brody leaned back in his chair but didn't let go of her hand.

"I'm not trying to be difficult or deny what you're saying," she clarified. "I'm just trying to understand."

"I know. And it's hard because it means there's just so much more to explain. You see, the Glenwood pack is kind of old-fashioned. We still carry on a lot of the traditions that more modern packs don't bother with. Like worshipping Selene... and marking our mates." He leaned up and scooted closer now, his hand drifting up her arm until he touched the curve between her neck and shoulder. "The male will use his fangs to bite the female, just here, and it deepens the bond between them. Once they have sex after marking, their bond is complete. Other wolves can see and scent the mark, but it also allows the couple to feel each other's strongest emotions."

"He marks her," Robin repeated back. "He claims her as his."

"In a way, but it's more than that," Brody insisted.

Robin swallowed. She wasn't upset about being mates. She knew that being with Brody was the right thing. It was the only thing. She didn't want to think about dating someone else or slowing down their relationship, whether they were wolves or humans.

But this marking thing was something else. A sense of desperation prickled her skin, the same sort of anxiety she used to get when JC would call her and demand to know where she was and who she was with. Logic told her that this wasn't the same thing and Brody would never treat her like that. It was impossible to forget the way things had been with JC, though, and she'd fought so hard to get away.

She felt like the newly tattooed bird on her hip was getting shoved right back into its cage.

14

BRODY PULLED UP IN FRONT OF THE PACKHOUSE. THE place was busy for a Monday. Some of the younger wolves had gotten together in the backyard for a bonfire. He could see them around the edge of the garage, talking and laughing. A few of them had snuck off into the shadows to make out. Someone's marshmallow had caught fire, which caused another round of laughter.

"Feeling wistful of your younger days, son?" Jimmy Glenwood came out of the garage, wiping the grease from his hands on a rag that already looked too greasy to do any good.

"Not exactly, but maybe wishing I'd done things differently back then." Brody turned away from the young wolves he'd spent so much time training and stepped into the garage with his father. "I've been thinking about that a lot lately, actually."

"No room in life for regrets, you know." Jimmy turned down the volume on one of his numerous old rockabilly albums he had playing and nudged his thumb toward the speaker. "I figure you're like old Carl Perkins here."

"That's a new one for me," Brody commented. He could appreciate his father's taste in music, though he'd never shared it.

"Well, Carl Perkins wrote a little song you might know called 'Blue Suede Shoes.' There are a few different stories floating around about exactly why he wrote it and what influenced him, but that doesn't really matter. The fact is that he did, and then he recorded it."

Brody leaned against the hefty toolbox, waiting patiently for this to go somewhere and make sense.

"He did pretty darn well with it, too. It was climbing the charts in Memphis, and then it was hitting the national charts. Right as things were starting to look big for him, he had a car accident and landed himself in the hospital. That made things difficult for him, for sure. The thing is, a lot of other guys on the same record label had also recorded the song. One of them, as you might know, was Elvis Presley."

"So then Elvis got all the money and credit?" Brody guessed, still not sure what direction this was supposed to be going.

"In the long run, sure. But the thing is, Elvis knew Carl Perkins. He recorded the song under the condition that it wouldn't be released as a single while Perkins' version was still doing well. Like I said, that auto accident meant old Carl was stuck in a hospital bed, and he started slipping from the spots he'd earned on the charts. But once Elvis got out there with it, it kept enough interest in the song that he was able to get a gold record." Jimmy winked and picked up a wrench.

"Okay. You got me. What the hell does that all mean?" Brody looked over the old wreck his father was working on. This one was bad enough that it wasn't easily identifiable, and he didn't pretend to know what it was.

Jimmy laughed and adjusted his glasses before he leaned in under the hood. "Well, if Carl Perkins hadn't written 'Blue Suede Shoes,' then it couldn't have been one of Elvis's first hits. Now he was talented, of course, and he was bound to take off one way or another, but Carl made a huge difference in that man's life. Elvis's is the one that people remember the most today, but they might not have if it weren't for Carl."

"I figure it's kind of the same for you and Devin," Jimmy continued. "That boy needed love and support, and you were there for him. He and his mother have moved on to do other things, but you can't underestimate the impression and influence that you had on his life. It was because of you that the boy had food on the table and a roof over his head. It was because of you that he knew so much before he even started school. I know it's pained your heart ever since they left, but don't shortchange yourself and start thinking you should've done something different. You did exactly what you were meant to."

Brody straightened as he listened. Leave it up to his father to know he was thinking about Devin even when he hadn't said it. "I never really thought about it like that. I've always just felt bad that I haven't been there for him all along."

"No, but you tried. And once the boy is old enough to make his own decisions, you can try again sometime. We all get hurt sometimes, but I don't want you to get all hung up on it. Ah! Got the old son of a bitch!" Jimmy straightened with a rusty bolt in his hand. "That sucker has been holding me up for the last hour."

"Thanks, Dad. I'm heading in to find Dawn."

"Anytime, son. Anytime. Next time you'll have to grab a wrench and help, though!" Jimmy's laughter followed him into the house.

Brody stopped in the kitchen for a soda. Something was simmering on the stove, and it smelled delicious. He peeked in the pot before he headed down the hall. There was wisdom in what his father had said. He could learn the lessons of the past, but he couldn't let himself get so caught up in it that he couldn't see the future. Maybe Devin had left a hole in his heart, and maybe there was no guarantee of ever having children with Robin, but things would work out the way they were supposed to. Shifters were big on fate, after all.

The problem was that he wasn't so sure Robin believed in it the same way he did.

When he peeked into the living room, he found Dawn and Lori sitting on the oversized comfy couch, each with a glass of wine in hand. "Am I interrupting?" he asked.

Dawn waved him into the room enthusiastically. "Not at all! We're just having some girl time. Oh, I keep forgetting to tell you that your test results came back. Everything was fine, just like you figured. I like having a fellow wolf in the hospital's lab, so I don't have to worry about anything weird getting flagged."

Lori frowned. "I didn't think about that. I swear, every day that goes by, I'm still learning more and more about being a shifter."

"Speaking of," Dawn began with a curious look, "how is the newest addition to the pack? And when will we get to meet her?"

Brody hadn't intended to sit down and chat, but now he collapsed into an armchair. As he felt the soft upholstery around him, he realized just how exhausting this had all been. "Fine, I guess. I'm not really even sure."

"Uh oh. Trouble in paradise?" Dawn asked.

He let out a long sigh. "Not trouble, exactly. It's more like paradise is up in the air once again, and I'm never sure if or where it's going to come back down again."

"You're being about as clear as Dad is when he's trying to explain something," Dawn noted.

Lori leaned forward to set her glass of wine on the coffee table and grabbed some cheese and crackers from the charcuterie board. "I assume you went and talked to her?"

"I did," he admitted. "I didn't give her as much

time as I'd meant to, partly because I was worried she could end up the next woman found in the woods and partly because I just couldn't stay away. She wasn't thrilled to see me, and I couldn't blame her. Then I showed her how to shift and protect herself." He laughed as he rubbed his thumb over his lip. "We were outside half the night, and she did pretty well by the end."

"So what's wrong, then? That sounds great. I, for one, won't mind having another woman around here. Does she like wine?" Dawn leaned back into the chair and grinned at her brother. "She can drink whatever she wants to. Just let her know that she's invited."

"I might, but I don't think she's ready to meet all of you." Brody propped his elbow on the arm of the chair and laid his head in his hand. "I'm worried I scared her off yesterday when we went out. There's a lot that the two of us have to talk about, and it's not always comfortable, but we were having a good time. Then she started telling me how she felt and describing this pull she has toward me."

"That's not a surprise if she provoked your wolf enough to nip her in the first place," Dawn noted.

"Yes, but she didn't understand what all of that meant because I hadn't told her about mates yet. So I

did. I tried to explain it all to her, along with marking. I don't think I did a very good job of it because
she kind of shut down after that. I asked her if
anything was wrong, and she said no, but the rest of
the date definitely wasn't the same." He'd been able
to feel just how much distance there was between
them after that, and it'd been bothering him ever
since. They'd made so much progress, only to slide
back again.

"To be fair, all of that is a lot to swallow," Lori
said gently. "It sounds to me like she started to feel
like she knew who she was and could understand
this whole wolf thing, but mating and marking is a
whole different aspect. I was a little unsure about it
myself at first."

Brody rubbed a hand over his face. "To me, it's
just a tiny part of something much bigger we might
have going on."

"Because you grew up with that knowledge," Lori
pointed out. "You've been a wolf your whole life. You
know about these things the same way humans
know about wedding dresses and throwing a
bouquet. It's just part of the ritual."

"That's a really good point," Dawn agreed. "We
probably don't think about it that much."

"I told her so she could be prepared," Brody tried

to explain. "Of course, that's also what I thought I was doing when I explained she would turn into a wolf. I just keep driving her away every time I try."

"Be patient with her," Lori advised gently. "I didn't know anything about my heritage, and I still have a hard time wrapping my head around it. Sometimes I look in the mirror and wonder how there can really be a wolf inside there, yet I'm living with it every day."

Brody pulled in a breath and let it out through his nose. He didn't mind if Robin wanted to wait a while before they furthered their relationship. He just didn't want her to decide she couldn't handle it and leave him. He needed to get to the point of knowing that things would be all right. "I'll try."

Dawn reached over and put a hand on his leg. "Don't give up on her, Brody. I know you've been hurt before. I can still see the worry of that all over your face. Robin is different."

He looked up, giving her some side-eye. "How would you know? You haven't met her."

"No," Dawn laughed, "but she's got to be one hell of a woman if she can get Brody Glenwood to worry about something. You let us know when she's coming over for some drinks and girl time." His sister winked at him.

"In the meantime, are you staying for dinner tonight? I've got my spaghetti sauce simmering in the kitchen," Lori said.

His stomach growled, responding for itself. "I guess I am. I'm just going to grab my sketchbook." He got up and headed out, fetching the book and his custom pencil case from the pencil bag. As he straightened, he looked up at the house.

This was where he'd grown up. This was where his family was from, a family that had loved and supported him. He hadn't always felt as though he fit in, but he was starting to realize he was less of an outsider than he'd thought. His father was right in telling him not to get caught up in the past. Dawn and Lori were right in advising him to be patient as he waited for the future.

He could only hope that he and Robin would find a way to make this work.

15

"THERE'S HARDLY BEEN A THING FOR ME TO DO HERE," Robin said with a smile as she wrapped things up with her last patient of the day. "You're doing such a great job brushing and flossing that we're actually going to finish the appointment early. Keep up the good work."

"Don't give me too much credit," the young man said as he sat up and swung his legs down to the floor. "I only do it because I'm afraid of having to get drilled again."

Robin laughed at his honesty. "Your secret's safe with me."

She brought him out to the front desk, where she saw Maggie leaning over her keyboard with her hand pressed to her forehead. "Are you okay?"

"Hm?" Maggie straightened, looking at her with bleary eyes. "I'm just not feeling all that well this afternoon."

Robin flicked her fingers at her. "You go on home, then. I can get him checked out."

"I don't want you to have to do that," Maggie replied.

"Don't be silly," Robin insisted. It was clear that Maggie was barely hanging on. Her skin was pale, her eyes were bloodshot, and she was moving slowly. "You're only going to miss the last half hour. I won't tell Watson," she added quietly as she moved around behind the counter.

"Okay. I think he's still got a patient back there, though." Maggie reached into the drawer to grab her purse.

"I can take care of it, and I'll cover for you." Robin knew as long as things were being handled, Watson wouldn't care if Maggie was behind the counter or 'in the bathroom' when his assistant Barb brought his patient up to the front.

There was, of course, plenty of cleaning to do at the end of the day. Robin spent a few minutes straightening out the waiting room, putting magazines back where they belonged, and shutting off the television. She was finding that her wolf had given her a strange new sense of energy and purpose. The slog of daily life had turned into an eager determination to get things done and see what was around the next corner. It was a good feeling, one she could definitely get used to. It didn't hurt that her wolf was becoming acclimated to the sensory overload that came with the dental office.

Robin grabbed the broom out of the supply closet and started on the floors in the back. The problem with the whole wolf thing was that it wasn't as simple as just having more energy and better vision. Those were a plus, but the rest still bothered her.

She frowned at the small pile of dirt forming in the middle of the hallway as her mind turned once again to her last date with Brody. He had been sweet and polite. She loved the way he genuinely expressed himself. So many people were trying to be someone they weren't just to look good, but he wasn't like that. There were days he wanted a burger at a little restaurant, and days he wanted to smell the fresh herbs at the farmer's market and cook at home. It was so very real.

Just like the fact he was a wolf, and that he'd made her one.

Just like the fact he believed they were destined to be together and that he'd mark her as his own.

Sweeping the dirt into the dustpan and pitching it into the trash, Robin moved to the front office to start in there. Barb escorted their last patient up to be checked out.

"Thanks, Robin. You don't mind if I head out in a sec, do you? I've got to go to my son's concert tonight, and I don't want to be late."

"Of course. It's pretty quiet tonight, so I'll handle closing up."

Once Robin dismissed their last patient, she picked up the broom again. This whole marking thing pushed its way back to the front of her brain. It was part of Brody's culture, something that was now about to be a part of her own culture. She was one of them now. It was the way things were done, yet Robin couldn't quite accept it. The issue wasn't with the bite itself, nor the blood that would inevitably be drawn.

No, it went much deeper than that.

As much of an asshole as he'd been to her, it hadn't been easy to leave JC. She'd known for a long time that she'd wanted out, yet the logistics and the what-ifs had stopped her. How would she pay for the house and bills on her own? What if he fought her on it and wouldn't let her out? What if it led to a long, dragged-out court battle simply because he wanted to make things difficult? It wasn't like he'd wanted things to work out. He'd refused to go to any kind of counseling when she'd still been trying to make things better between them, and he certainly hadn't changed his ways. But he was a stubborn jerk, and he would hurt her as much as he could if it meant it preserved his sense of manhood.

In the end, he hadn't put up much of a fight. He'd pretended, here and there, saying he wanted the washer and dryer, the television, or the china that had belonged to Robin's grandmother. Finally, Robin had fisted her hands at her sides and told him he could have every scrap in the house as long as he was out of it. That'd been the final blow. He hadn't argued for anything further, and he'd only taken what was rightfully his.

Robin quirked one side of her mouth up. It was easy to summarize it all and break it down into one simple story, but the emotional journey she'd been on that entire time had been far bigger and more desperate than a few visits with an attorney and a quick court date could account for. She'd set herself free. She had a chance to do what she wanted with her life, to be herself without having to account for someone else.

In her heart, she knew that things would be different with Brody, no matter what. He'd already proven he wasn't trying to change her, at least not any more than he already had. That was an accident, and in many ways, Robin had no regrets about it.

Grumbling to herself, she finished the front desk area and moved into Watson's office. She could go back and forth with herself all day and all night, and still, she wouldn't come to a conclusion. Part of the problem was that this was a matter of the heart. It couldn't be solved by simple logic or even complicated logic. She couldn't make a choice based on what made sense. She had to go with what she felt, and figuring that out was harder than it ought to be.

Starting by the window and working her way toward the door, Robin's mind continued to churn as she swept. She wanted to come to some sort of decision. It would at least mean she could relax for a little while, and that was something she needed badly. Wouldn't it be nice to just enjoy her time with Brody? To lean into whatever they had going on between them, fated or not? The thought filled her with warmth. Maybe she'd been thinking about this too hard.

The odd tension on the broom made her look down. A thin red band of leather had come out from underneath Watson's desk. Robin repositioned the broom and tried to pull it the rest of the way out. It was hung up on something, though. Trying again, Robin managed to pull out about another inch and paused to look down at it for a moment. This definitely wasn't anything she normally swept out from under the furniture. It looked like a purse strap.

Curious, Robin reached down and gave it a good yank with her hand. The bottom drawer of the desk rattled as a slim purse came flying out. It whipped around Robin's hand like a boomerang, sending the contents skittering out of the open zipper.

Her heart jumped into her throat. Whatever this was, she had a feeling she wasn't meant to find it. Watson had all sorts of women coming in and out of this office. Had one of his flings left her purse there, and he'd stuffed it away to hide the proof of his entanglement? Robin wouldn't doubt if he brought them in back-to-back, insisting to each woman that she was the only one he was interested in.

Whatever it meant, she knew she couldn't just leave it all there. Robin quickly picked up a tube of lipstick and a collapsible hairbrush and stuffed them back into the purse. She had to step over to the window to reach the wallet. When she turned it over, she saw that the owner's driver's license was slipped into a clear pocket on the outside. It was none of her business, and she just needed to put it all back together and get the hell out of there. But her curiosity got the better of her, and she held it for a moment.

Sienna Barry. Robin frowned, wondering why the name was so familiar. She studied the smiling photo of a young, attractive woman who'd somehow managed to get a decent driver's license photo. She was a patient, Robin remembered. She'd seen her in the office before.

That was all perfectly logical. People met with Watson in his office all the time to discuss options and payment plans. There was no reason someone couldn't have left their purse in there. Robin had occasionally left her own purse in a restaurant or at a friend's house. But her throat closed when she realized the name wasn't familiar just because it was in their computers.

This was the most recent woman who'd been found dead in the woods.

She desperately wanted to be wrong. Robin pulled her phone out of her pocket, her fingers shaking as she tried to find the news story to verify what she saw.

"It's all very simple, really, and we've got to do something. You have to admit that I've done more than my fair share of—"

Robin's entire body jerked as footsteps and voices sounded in the doorway behind her. She turned to find her boss staring at her. He looked at the wallet in her hand and then up at her face, his eyes quickly turning angry. She was caught, and she knew it. The gush of adrenaline in her system told her to run, that things were more horrifically wrong than she could ever imagine, yet there was nowhere to go.

A woman stood just behind Watson, tall and slim, with perfect skin and judgmental eyes. Robin had seen her before. Running on high speed, Robin's brain flickered to another day when this woman had been in the office recently. Edith, she'd said her name was. She was one of Watson's pompous friends.

Her boss would be furious with her for calling him out right in front of one of his people, but Robin wasn't going to wait around until it was convenient for him. "Why do you have this?" she demanded.

"What the hell are you doing with that?" Watson asked simultaneously.

Edith gestured so quickly that it made Robin flinch. She rolled her hand through the air and formed a fist in front of her face. When she uncurled her fingers and blew on her palm, thousands of glittering green crystals filled the air and headed straight for Robin.

Flinching instinctively, Robin stepped back. There was no place for her to go, no escape to be had. The glittering particles filled her mouth and nose and choked her. Robin's vision darkened around the edges until she could only see what was directly in front of her. She dropped the wallet and leaned against the desk, finding that her feet didn't want to stay underneath her. That disc of vision continued to telescope smaller and smaller. Her arms and legs were numb now, leaving only her tremulous heartbeat. Fear had taken over her completely. Robin knew she should be doing something, but her mind refused to let her know what. She slid to the floor, only vaguely aware of the cold linoleum beneath her. Two faces appeared in the last remnants of her vision as Watson and Edith peered down at her.

"I think that'll do," Watson said with finality.

16

"LORI, I KNOW YOU AND I WERE DESTINED TO BE together, but I would've taken you as my mate for this spaghetti alone." Rex shook his head in pleasure as he twirled another big bite onto his fork.

"Is that really all it takes to find a man?" Dawn asked. "Lori, you and I are going to have to spend some time in the kitchen. I need some lessons."

"Pass the parmesan?"

"Max, you're not even going to be able to taste it under all that cheese!" Joan chided, though she smiled as she passed the dish of hand-grated parmesan to her son.

"Cheese makes everything better," Jimmy countered. "Pass me that when you're done, son."

"Is there any more garlic bread?" Hunter asked.

"I'll get the rest out of the kitchen." Lori, looking delighted, went to fetch it.

Her son Conner gave Hunter a challenging look. "I'll wrestle you for the garlic bread."

"You will not!" Lori called back from the kitchen.

Brody ate slowly and thoughtfully. His family was all there, and he ought to be enjoying the moment. With their varying schedules, they couldn't always manage to have dinner together. His parents had retired from pack leadership once Rex had taken over as Alpha. Rex was always busy, whether he was running the pack or his rock club, Selene's. As his Luna, Lori shared those same responsibilities with him. Max's position at the club meant he was usually there any time Rex couldn't be. Dawn worked long, relentless shifts at the hospital, and half the time, she never knew exactly when she'd be off. Hunter and Conner were about the only ones that Brody got to spend quality time with on a regular basis, and that was only because he'd been training the younger wolves. This was the perfect time for him to catch up, but he wasn't quite feeling it.

"Have you heard anything back from Kane?" Lori asked when she returned to the table. She pointed her finger at the two boys. "And there's plenty for everyone."

Rex shrugged. "The police are on it, but nothing new has come to light. They don't have any good leads, at least not until some results come back from the lab."

"It's strange, isn't it?" Dawn commented. "Everything is quiet and peaceful, then all of a sudden, two bodies are found in the woods. I hope it's making the young women in Eugene pay attention to their surroundings and stay in groups. I see plenty of bad things happening with the patients at the hospital, and I don't like to think it could be getting worse."

"Maybe someone is trying to send a message," Max speculated. He continued when Rex looked at him with interest. "They were both found on our territory."

"True," Rex acknowledged, "but you also have to consider that our territory is pretty damn big. The fact that it includes the park and some of the other surrounding woods means that this could be pure coincidence. I don't want to jump to conclusions and take this personally unless we find that we have a good reason."

"If it were a message, it would make more sense for these victims to be people we know," Brody pointed out absently as he poked his fork into his spaghetti. "Either that or someone's just shitty at sending messages."

"You did say that you'd tattooed the most recent one," Max pointed out.

Brody had to acknowledge the truth of that. "Yes, but not the first one. I'd never seen her before." He'd considered that same notion himself, and he'd been grateful to be able to dismiss it.

"Listen to all of you," Joan said, sitting back and touching the crystal that hung around her neck. "You're here having dinner with your family, but you sound like you're having a pack meeting."

"Isn't it great?" Jimmy grinned.

She playfully slapped her mate on the arm. "You were just as bad back in your day. Business is important, but they need time to rest, too."

As his parents continued to argue the finer points of scheduling pack business, Brody's wolf grew urgent inside him. He brushed it off. He hadn't been able to stop thinking about Robin, and discussing the recent murders hadn't helped. He was just in a sensitive frame of mind at the moment; there was no need to panic. But the more he tried to push it away, the more his wolf insisted. Adrenaline shot through him, and his heart raced. Something was wrong. Terribly wrong.

"Excuse me for a second." Scraping his chair back, Brody stepped out onto the back patio and whipped his phone out of his pocket. He dialed Robin's number. Everyone else he cared about was right there in front of him, and there was no denying that he had a deep connection with her. They might not have yet completed their bond, but the beginnings of it were certainly in place.

The line rang and rang before going to voicemail. Brody hung up and tried again with the same result. He double-checked the time, and now his stomach was in knots.

Everyone was looking at him when he stepped back into the kitchen. "Robin isn't answering her phone."

"Maybe she had to work late," Lori reasoned.

Brody shook his head. "Not this late. I'm going by her house to check on her." For someone who was supposed to be giving her space and time to mull over their relationship, he was doing a piss poor job. Right now, though, he didn't particularly care. He'd never forgive himself if he ignored his beast and something happened to his mate.

"Darling, let me save you a trip." Joan got up from the table and came around until she stood in front of Brody. "Things might be fine, but I can locate her so you'll know for sure. Do you have anything of hers?"

His wolf didn't want to wait while Joan worked her magic. It wanted to go and see Robin for itself. But Brody knew just how strong his mother's powers were. If she could find Robin, he'd be able to get to her faster, even if she was just at home. "Um, oh. Here. I have these." He grabbed her reading glasses out of the pocket of his flannel, the same one he'd worn on their date the day before. He'd nearly forgotten about them until now.

"Perfect. Just give me a minute." Joan moved over to the patio door, her dark skirt swishing around her legs. She pulled in several deep breaths as she looked up at the moon, and Brody could hear her mutter a quiet prayer to Selene. Pressing her elbows to her sides, she put her hands in front of her and held Robin's glasses in the cradle of her palms.

The clock on the dining room wall ticked loudly with every passing second, sending a sense of urgency through Brody. He gritted his teeth and forced himself to be still to avoid interrupting her spell. This was supposed to save him time, but it didn't quite feel like it at the moment. Brody's wolf reeled inside him, desperate for him to get the hell out the door and over to Robin's place. He'd be warring with himself forever until he had Robin in his sights.

Joan pulled in a slow, deep breath. Her eyes remained closed, and when she spoke, it was so quiet that Brody had to step closer to hear her. "She's in town, but she's not close."

"What does that mean?" He took another step, wishing he could dive into his mother's vision and see for himself.

"Mmm," was her only answer for the moment.

Dawn was next to him now. "Just give her a minute," she whispered. "She'll get there. It just takes a bit to hone in, especially on someone she's never met before."

"The other side of town," Joan said, a little stronger now. "I can see a home. It's big. Old. Prestigious. The kind with towers and a lot of fancy trim. Like a Victorian mansion or something."

His patience was growing so thin it was barely in existence anymore. Architectural details weren't going to help him much. "What's she doing there?" He wasn't even sure if that was something she could tell him.

Joan's face during the entire process had been

peaceful and serene as she'd focused in on her abilities. Now her brow furrowed, and she frowned. Tiny muscles in her face began to twitch, and every movement sent a bump of fear through his heart. Brody pressed his tongue against the roof of his mouth, fighting the urge to question her more than he already had.

"She's being held." His mother's words were quick and angry. "She can't leave, but she wants to. I can feel that in her."

"Held?" His wolf was going wild now, thrashing and clawing. He didn't know what any of this meant, but he had to find out. "By who?"

His mother's face crumpled further. She looked like she was in pain, but she didn't break her stance or her concentration. "There's a powerful witch. She's young, yet she's not. She has a very strange energy about her, one that I don't like even from a distance. Whatever she's up to, it isn't any good."

"Anyone you know?"

Her head gave a quick shake of insult. "Definitely not."

"Tell me where," Brody growled.

"On the west side of town, but it's wooded. There's enough cover to get there on all fours without getting into the streets." Joan opened her eyes.

He'd inherited his hazel coloring from her, but he hoped the fear he saw there wasn't reflected in his own eyes. He sure as hell didn't feel it inside. Anger, rage, and a tremendous desire to protect Robin, but definitely not fear. "I'm going to fucking destroy her."

"We all will." Rex put his hand on Brody's shoulder.

Brody hadn't even realized that everyone else had stood. They were there with him, waiting for the information as though she were a member of their own family. Robin was, in a way, but they hadn't even met her yet. "You don't have to do that."

"Don't start with that," Rex advised. "You know that's not how we do things around here. Mom will lead the way since she knows where Robin is. Max, it's up to you whether or not you want Hunter to come along."

"I'm ready," Hunter told his father. They could all see the light that shone in his eyes, the one that said not only was he ready for battle physically but emotionally, too.

Max gave him a nod. "Fine. You stay at my back and don't be a hero. That's Brody's job."

Without much more discussion, they were out the back door. Brody didn't hesitate to allow his wolf to take over. It came on more quickly than usual and sprang to life as he ran, his feet leaving the ground as human and coming down as paws. The others flooded behind him, their movements so soft, they could only be heard by each other. The moon was full and bright overhead, a promising sign.

Brody lifted his head just long enough to soak up some of that special moonlight, and he hoped it would be enough to get him through this.

17

ROBIN SAT STARING AT THE WOLF. IT WAS BEAUTIFUL, and she felt like she'd seen it before. It sat peacefully across from her in this dark space, its fluffy tail wrapped around its paws. It regarded her with its gold eyes, slanting up slightly at the outside corners. The wolf knew something, but it wasn't going to tell her what that was. It got up and ran off into the darkness.

She tried to call out to the wolf, but her voice didn't work. She wanted to run after it, so she wouldn't be alone, but her body wouldn't work either. Robin sat frozen where she was. Wherever *this* was. Everything was so confusing.

Pain pounded through the blackness, thudding off the walls and reverberating through her brain.

Robin fought against it, trying to figure out how to drive it back, but the pain was so heavy.

"She's starting to come to."

The voice was familiar, but it made her want to shrink back into the unknown. She found she couldn't, though. Consciousness pulled harder than the darkness did. As she roused, she realized the walls the pain had been ricocheting off of were actually the inside of her skull. Her eyelids were so heavy that it hurt to lift them.

"I'm not sure why I'm bothering." This voice, a female's, wasn't familiar. "She's a bit old and barely worth the trouble."

She managed to get her eyes open enough that she could see, but it didn't help. The room was dim, lit only by a weak, flickering light. The floor was hard beneath her. The last floor she remembered seeing was white linoleum. This was old hardwood, and it hurt as it pressed hard against one side of her body.

"I'm sure she'll be fine," the first voice replied testily. "It's not like we haven't given him plenty of other younger ones."

"Don't claim to understand his needs better than I do!" the woman snapped. "You wouldn't have the benefit of all that he's given you without me!"

Robin tried to move her hands to get them underneath her. The hard floor wasn't helping anything. Things would be better if she could just sit up. She managed to move her fingers, but the rough scraping of rope around her wrists kept her from doing more. Automatically, she tried her feet with the same result. Panic bloomed in Robin's chest. She still didn't understand where she was or what was going on, but it couldn't be good if her arms and legs were bound.

"Ah, finally decided to join us?" Dr. Watson's face loomed in her vision. His cold eyes sparked with evil as he watched her twist in pain.

"What..." Her tongue was thick and dry in her mouth. "What's going on?" she managed to ask.

"Maybe you should sit up, look around, and find out for yourself." His hand clamped her arm and yanked her upright so that she sat on the floor. He pushed her, turning her partially.

Robin now understood why the light was flickering and dim. It came only from a ring of crimson candles standing on the floor. She didn't recognize where she was as she took in the tall ceilings and old wallpaper. Carved wooden furniture had been pushed out of the way to make enough room for the circle of candles.

And in the middle of that circle, a woman stood. She bent and placed something on the floor near the perimeter, and only once she moved out of the way did Robin see that it was a glass jar. It was filled with a murky substance that Robin couldn't identify, and she thought she saw something moving inside it.

Her eyes lifted to the woman. She was elegant but had the harsh look of someone who was easily displeased. Robin's fuddled mind refused to cooperate, though she knew she'd seen her before. She looked back up at Dr. Watson in confusion.

Putting his hands on his hips, he tipped back his head and smirked. "For someone who likes to cause as much trouble as you, I thought you would've already figured this out. After all, you already know I've been writing illegal prescriptions for those willing to pay my price. You already turn your nose up every time I give one of my friends the privileges they deserve. So what's wrong now, Robin? You truly have no idea what's happening?"

None of this made sense. Robin shook her head.

"I'm more than happy to explain it to you. Have you ever wondered, Robin, how I managed to build my business the way I have? Haven't you ever wondered what made so many people flock to me for their dental needs when there are plenty of other dentists in the area?" He lifted his hands in the air.

"Advertising? Because it certainly wasn't your sparkling personality." Fear was still reigning in her body, but anger was beginning to bubble to the surface. She didn't understand anything yet, but Watson was obviously in on it.

"I'd advise you to drop that attitude if it mattered. Or at least, it won't for long. You see, Edith and I have been working together for quite some time." He gestured toward the woman.

Robin turned back to her, watching her scatter a thin layer of fine dust in between the candles. Edith. Right. The woman that had been with Watson back at the office.

"Business is all about connections, and Edith has just the one I needed. The dark lord she serves is incredibly powerful and can make all sorts of things happen. All we've had to do is provide him with the life force of young women, and in return, he bestows us the gifts of youth and success."

It was all too much, and Robin's mind reeled. First, she discovered the existence of wolf shifters, and that she was becoming one herself. Now there were witches and sacrifices to a dark lord? She shook her head as she tried to understand, but the headache left from whatever Edith had done to her was still lingering. "Wouldn't it have been safer for you to just get some Botox and pay for more of your tacky TV ads?"

"You obviously don't have a mind for business, Robin. And speaking of Botox, you should've started that a long time ago. Those crows feet and laugh lines aren't doing you any favors." Watson shook his head and pouted his lips. "Just dreadful."

"Fuck my wrinkles, asshole! What's dreadful is that you killed Sienna Barry." If he'd already told her this much, she wouldn't likely get out of this situation soon. Robin wanted to know the truth. If she had to die, too, then at least she wouldn't die ignorant.

"I did," Watson replied as easily as if they were discussing the weather. "She was young and cute, and she had so much life in her. She was the perfect sacrifice. You'll get to see it firsthand when it happens to you."

"You know, Albert, our sacrifices don't truly need to know what we're doing and why," Edith replied, her voice tired. "It takes all the fun out of it for me."

"Oh, but this is different," Watson insisted. He looked down at Robin once again. "This one's going to be particularly fun for *me*. You've always been a bit of a pain, Robin, but finding Sienna's purse is the last mistake you'll make."

"Someone is going to wonder where I am," Robin pointed out. She almost said something about Maggie, but she held her tongue. She didn't want to put anyone else in danger. "You can't just off people and expect no one to find out."

"They didn't until very recently," Watson countered calmly. "The boy I'd hired to dispose of the bodies got a little lazy and put two of them too close to each other. I took care of him, and now I'll take care of you. Is it ready yet, Edith?"

The witch scowled at him as she pulled something withered out of a burlap sack and placed it on the floor in the center of the circle. "You know it isn't."

"Fine, fine. What can I help you with so we can get this done, then?" Watson, confident of the bindings that held Robin, stepped toward Edith.

Robin racked her mind, trying to figure out what she should do. She obviously couldn't just get up and walk out of there, though it was something she clearly should've done at her job a long time ago. No one else was around, at least not that she knew of. The heavy curtain on the window off to the left was partially open. In the moonlight, she could see that this house was in the middle of the woods. There was no chance of a neighbor hearing her scream if she tried that tactic.

Lifting her eyes, Robin focused on the bright sphere in the sky. The moon and its goddess, Selene, Brody had called her. She hadn't had the chance to ask him much more about that whole idea, but she was finding that she liked it. Selene was beautiful and calming as she shed her light over the night world. Robin felt her wolf stir inside her.

Her wolf. She realized now that she'd seen it when she was still out. The wolf she'd been sitting across from was herself. She'd dive into self-analysis later, but right now, there was a chance her wolf could help. Robin was stronger when she was in that form, and her ankles and wrists were a different shape and size. Maybe it would give her some sort of chance of escape. If Watson and Edith were thrown off by suddenly having a wolf in the room, so much the better.

Remembering her lesson with Brody and wishing they'd taken the time to squeeze in more of them, Robin took in a deep breath. She let it out slowly, trying to release her human form and let the wolf take over. She felt it there, just under the surface. It was close and coming closer. She kept her eyes closed to block out the room, willing this creature inside her to come out. The underside of her skin began to itch violently, and an aching like the middle of winter filled her bones. Just a little more, and she'd have it.

But nothing happened. Frustrated, Robin looked down at her body. It was still very much human.

Shit. What was it Brody had said? She had to let down her own defenses. That made sense. It was scary to turn into something else, to become a different creature than she'd been her entire life. Plus, it hurt like hell while it was happening. All she had to do was relax.

No matter how many deep breaths she attempted, though, Robin didn't make any progress. She leaned forward and pressed her head to the floor. She was too nervous, and there was no way she couldn't be when she was about to be killed. Not just killed but sacrificed to some dark lord. Her guts swirled inside her.

So did regret. At the time, it'd seemed that discovering she was becoming a wolf shifter was the strangest thing that'd ever happened to her. Being sacrificed, Robin decided, definitely topped the list over that one. What good had it done to train in wolf form if she couldn't even become one? What good had it done her to stay at an unsatisfying job when the bills she'd been so worried about paying were about to become obsolete?

And what good had it done to start her life over when it was all about to be taken away?

Her heart wrapped around thoughts of Brody. She'd doubted him on numerous levels. She'd pulled away from him when she thought he'd asked too much of her. Robin realized that even though she'd pushed away, come back, and then pushed away again, Brody had been right there for her the entire time. She'd been a fool to suddenly balk. If she hadn't, maybe the two of them would've had a chance to spend a little more time together.

The loud thump that suddenly ripped through the room startled Robin upright. Her muscles tightened, and she jerked painfully against her bonds. She swiveled her head around, trying to see what was happening.

Edith and Watson turned as well. "What the hell is that?" Edith demanded.

She got her answer when another resounding crash went through the room. The candles flickered as the door banged open, sending pieces of intricately carved trim splintering to the floor. The doorway filled with gray fur as several wolves came charging into the room. They surrounded her captors, their hackles raised and their teeth bared.

A woman rushed in after them. Her curly gray hair hung down her back, and the skirt of her dark purple dress whisked around her legs. Her brilliant hazel eyes flared as she curled her hand through the air and then whipped it forward, sending a ball of flame shooting from her fingertips.

Robin watched it all in pure disbelief. Was she dreaming this? Was she hoping so badly for a rescue that her poor, addled brain had allowed her the illusion of one just to make her feel better in her final moments?

"Robin."

"Brody!" Her heart soared at the sight of him, but she still wasn't quite sure she could believe all of this. It was too wild to be true. "Is that really you? What's happening?"

His fingers worked quickly at her bonds, and he grinned. "I guess this is one heck of a way for you to meet my mother."

18

BRODY KEPT HIS WOLF IN CHECK WHILE HE FREED Robin from the last of her bonds, but it wasn't easy. He'd felt the urgency of getting to her with every pump of his blood as they'd raced to this strange mansion in the woods. That had only magnified once they'd found her. They'd decided as a pack that the witches would go in on two feet to make the most of their powers. He wouldn't be satisfied until he had Robin in his arms again. He did now, but seeing the deep gashes that the ropes had made in her wrists and ankles made a twist of rage run through him.

"You've got to get out of here," Robin urged as she held one hand in the other, trying to relieve her pain. "Edith. She's one of his friends, but she's a witch. She's the one who killed the other women, and I don't want anything to happen to you or your pack." Her eyes were wide as she tried to take in everything happening around her.

A screech filled the room, issued from the woman Robin had called Edith as she pressed her hands to her chest and then flung them forward. A vortex of blackness spun through the air toward Dawn. His sister dodged to the side as she summoned her own powers, but Brody saw the massive hole it left in the wall behind her.

"Don't worry about that," Brody reassured her, though he knew this wasn't a guaranteed mission despite the numbers being in their favor. Whoever this woman was, she was incredibly powerful. He forced himself to focus on Robin. There was no point in all of this if he didn't get her out of there. "I need you to shift."

Robin shook her head. "I can't. I already tried. I can't concentrate enough. Plus, she put some sort of spell on me, and I've still got this horrible pounding in my head."

He didn't doubt that was true. She'd hardly spent any time in wolf form so far, and he couldn't imagine trying to shift in such circumstances when she wasn't used to it. The aftereffects of a spell wouldn't help. "I know, but we'll get you out of here much faster if you're on four legs."

She clung to him as the fighting raged around them. Max and Conner had managed to get around behind Edith as she battled the others, and Max clamped his teeth around the back of her knee. The witch responded with a crackling surge of red energy from her fingertips that sent him and Conner flying back into the corner of the room. They smacked into the wall, breaking the plaster. An old frame above them teetered on its nail and then fell, scattering broken glass over their fur.

Meanwhile, Hunter had cornered Dr. Watson, his teeth bared and his hackles raised. He bunched his muscles and lunged. His size and strength were no match for the older man, but the iron curtain rod the doctor had snagged from a pile of junk in the corner was. He swung it like a baseball bat, sending Hunter flying back.

Brody could feel the uncertainty in Robin, and he knew he had to fix it somehow, or they'd never make it out of there. He took her face in his hands and forced her to look only at him. "If you shift, you'll heal faster. The headache will go away, and it'll be like the ropes were never around you. I need you to trust me on this, Robin." Her skin was gritty with dust, streaked by the traces of tears.

She swallowed, her breath quick and shallow. "I'll try, Brody. But I'm so worried about you."

He pushed his face closer to hers, hoping it was enough to drown out the rest of the room. "We've got this. *You've* got this. Just close your eyes and listen to the sound of my voice."

She flinched as something heavy fell to the floor just behind them.

"Take a deep breath. That's it. Just like that. Let it out. Let yourself relax. Everything is going to be okay. Your wolf is in there, and I have no doubt that it wants to come out right now." He knew his sure as hell did. Eventually, Robin would be able to call her creature forward in urgent times without even giving it more than a thought, but she wasn't there yet. "Another deep breath. Good. Remember how it felt to be in your wolf form when you and I were in your back-yard. Think about how good it felt to be in that skin."

The barest hint of a smile touched her lips.

"You want that back. I know you do. This whole thing will feel completely different when you bring your wolf back. It's new, I know. But you can do this." He licked his lips and pressed his forehead against her. They couldn't communicate telepathically in their human form, but nevertheless, he willed all of his knowledge and experience into her. "Let everything else melt away, even yourself. Think about the sharpness of your teeth, the strength of your muscles, and the thickness of your fur. You need it, Robin. It needs you, too."

Her breathing had steadied, and she'd relaxed against him enough that he was holding her up. For a moment, Brody thought this might be another failed attempt, but a rippling of her skin suddenly brought out her fur. She writhed out of his hands and curled her arms and legs inward as pain moved through her body, but he knew this was a different type of pain than she'd been feeling.

"That's it," he coaxed as a new fear took over her eyes. "Good job, Robin. Just keep going. You're almost there."

Her head rolled on her shoulders, and a moan escaped her lips. Her body distorted and changed. The marks on her skin left by the ropes were quickly covered in fur. She stretched and shrunk, and then she was the breathtaking wolf he'd seen before.

Brody quickly made the change himself. He instantly felt Robin's presence in his mind, which comforted him deeply. He thought he sensed something else along with it for a moment, a glimmer of hope. *Good. I knew you could do it. Now let's get you out of here.*

No. Robin turned away from him and toward the fight. *I can't just leave. It's all my fault that this has happened.*

It's not. Brody circled around Robin to stand between her and the battle. *You can't take responsibility for this, Robin. It's just something that happened, and you got caught up in it.*

And me turning into a shifter was also just something that happened, something that wasn't your fault, she was quick to point out, taking a step back so she could look him directly in the eyes. *You didn't have to take as much responsibility for it as you did, but you wanted to make sure you did everything you could to make it right. Are you really going to tell me I can't do the same thing?*

He saw the challenge in her eyes just before they ducked to the side to avoid a brilliant fireball. Brody scrambled back to his feet. One of the fireballs had reached the curtains over the window, and the flames were quickly licking up the dense fabric. The old, dry wood of the house was the perfect fodder for the fire. Some of the candles on the floor had fallen over, their red wax pooling on the old wood.

Smoke accumulated near the tall ceiling. It was only a matter of time before they wouldn't be able to see what they were doing. Brody knew they couldn't stand around arguing about this. *Fine. Let's get all of us out of here, then.*

They joined the fray. Joan was whipping brilliant blue orbs as fast as she could, sending them like pulsing laser blasts at Edith. Sweat was beaded on her brow, and her shoulders were beginning to hunch. She was getting tired.

Dawn had stepped up beside her mother to assist. With her wrists together and her palms spread wide, she sent a blast of energy toward Edith. It was one that couldn't be seen, a hidden pulse that rippled through the air and couldn't be detected by the enemy until it was felt. Edith, however, had seen it coming. With a flick of her fingers, she sent it flying back. Dawn reeled over backward, hitting the floor with a thump.

"What the hell is happening?" Watson screamed as he took another swat with the curtain rod, which sent Rex staggering back for a moment.

"You were dumb enough to bring a shifter in here!" Edith replied as more lightning flashed from her fingers. She was trying to fight off Lori, who'd lept at her from in between Joan and Dawn and had gone for her throat. "We had only gone for humans for a reason!"

"As if I knew shifters were a thing!" Pure terror contorted Watson's face as he fought against Rex's next advance. He glanced to the side and saw that his path to the door was clear while everyone was so busy fighting. He darted for it. "I'm getting the fuck out of here!"

"The hell you are!" Edith swung around toward him, her eyes ablaze and her dark hair sticking to her forehead as she sent Watson tumbling to the ground. One more yank of her arm, and he was dragged backward across the floor, returning to the same corner where he'd started.

Brody could feel the anger and fear brewing in Robin's blood. He was shocked to see her race forward, leaping aside to avoid a candle as she barreled toward Watson. Her teeth gnashed the air, ready to get to him before he recovered his defenses.

Watson seemed to be running on panic and adrenaline. He recovered the curtain rod he'd used before and held it in front of him as Robin launched her first attack. It slammed her across the chest, but she stayed on her feet.

Brody was on her tail, not about to let her battle her first fight alone. There was little room for them to work and still avoid the flames and spells flying through the air. He felt the heat singeing the tips of his fur as he stepped up to fight at her side.

The two of them only had one training session together, yet it was clear that she'd retained everything he'd taught her. They darted in and back in unison, barely needing to communicate. If Watson went for one of them, the other attacked when he was occupied. Robin kept herself steady, prioritizing her balance and safety over her attacks. She was sure not to turn her back to Watson or give him any chance at her most vulnerable places.

Pride swelled through Brody's chest. If they didn't make it out of this alive, at least he'd know they died fighting together. The pull he'd felt for her had started when they'd first met, and it had only grown. Now, with both of them in their wolves and fighting for not just their own lives but those of their pack, he had no doubt the universe had put them together for a reason. She was his mate. He'd do whatever she needed so they could live that way at some point. If she wanted space and time to think, if she refused the mark, whatever. He'd spent too much time mulling over stupid things like that instead of just being with her. He could only hope that she felt the same intensity that rolled through him right now as his claws scraped the floor and he dove in for another strike.

Watson turned to defend himself from Brody. He still had the curtain rod in both hands, holding it out straight in front of him instead of swinging it around wildly. His movements were surprisingly quick as he warded off Brody's attacks. Brody moved to his left to try from there, and when Watson turned toward him and away from Robin, it gave him an idea. Though he knew he couldn't get through the man's defenses this way, Brody took another step to the left and tried again. Then again.

Robin saw the opening before Brody could even send her his thoughts. With Watson turned away from her, he'd done exactly what she'd been trained not to do and left his side unguarded. With all of Watson's attention on Brody, he didn't see Robin as she lunged. Her teeth flashed in the bright light of the glowing fire just before they sank into his neck.

His soft skin made a slight pop as it was punctured. Watson dropped the rod. It thudded to the floor and rolled away as he careened to the side. His hand pushed and punched at Robin, but they were no match for her. Blood sprayed out over her fur. Her muzzle wrinkled as she bit down harder, clamping her jaws as Watson swung back and forth.

His screams only came out as gurgles, choked with the blood that flooded his throat. His eyes widened and then dimmed before he slumped to the floor. Robin stepped back, blood dripping from her teeth.

There was no time to give her the accolades she deserved. Fire was consuming the room, and he felt his chest burning with every effort. Brody turned to the other half of the fight, looking for the right moment to dive in. Edith was strong, and she was determined. She screamed obscenities as she flung her powers left and right, sending blasts of energy bashing into the wolves that skirted her as Joan and Dawn continued their efforts. Brody could see their energy was fading, but he also saw the resolve on their faces.

Dawn dropped one hand, and for a moment, Brody thought she was about to give up. Instead, she rested it on her mother's shoulder. He understood then, and so did Joan. As the wolves gathered around the witch to keep her attacks coming at them, Dawn and Joan pressed their hands together. Energy crackled through the air, and Brody's fur stood on end as the power built. Their hands slowly separated, leaving an orb floating in the air between them. Fantastical colors swirled inside it, and it grew in size as their hands continued to separate. When it was ready, they flung it forward.

Edith turned just in time to see it coming at her, but it was too late. The orb crashed into her. She stumbled back, and the flame from a candle licked up the leg of her pants. She looked down and screamed. Another orb from Dawn and Joan sent her tumbling to the floor.

The flames crackled loudly, urging the Glenwoods to get out while they could, but they waited. Edith had been strong, and they couldn't risk her coming after any of them again. Brody stepped closer, ready to jump in with the first bite as soon as she so much as twitched. Instead, he watched as her lips puckered and dried. Her cheeks sank in, and a wash of gray, then white, moved through her dark hair. The firm muscles of her body turned to drooping flesh. Brody would've guessed her to be in her thirties, but in a matter of seconds, she rapidly moved through decades of aging. The wolves hung back as she shriveled into little more than a skeleton covered in skin, and the light in her eyes dulled. Her remaining flesh peeled back and disappeared, leaving nothing more than bones. Her frame crackled and fell, merely dust as it hit the floor.

Rex's thoughts reached out to the pack. *I think it's*

safe to say she won't be coming back for a rematch. Let's go.

With Joan and Dawn now in their wolf forms, the Glenwood pack flooded out into the hallways and down the stairs. The fire had spread and filled the house with smoke. Brody hadn't noticed the heat during the fight, but it pressed on him now. They broke out into the fresh night air and off across the overgrown lawn.

When they reached the edge of the woods, Robin stopped and looked back. Brody paused alongside her. He, too, turned to see the thick column of blackness rising into the night sky. He could swear that smoke was far darker than it should've been. The fire reflected in her eyes as he turned back to her. *Are you okay?*

Her inner voice was calmer than he expected. *I think I am. I didn't know I was capable of that. He told me that they'd killed the other women, the ones found in the woods. I was still kind of scared and confused when he was telling me about it, but I think he'd been doing it for a long time.*

Brody thought about the countless years that'd taken over the witch as she'd died. *You're probably right. It's all over now, thanks to you.*

Thanks to me? She leaned close to him. *You can't*

give me the credit here. I wouldn't have lived through that if it weren't for you and your pack.

That might've been true, but Brody's wolf still swelled with pride and contentment, knowing his mate had bravely fought with him side by side to remove the threat. He'd never been so in awe or in love.

19

BRODY WATCHED ROBIN CAREFULLY AS THEY ALL settled into the basement of the packhouse. Everyone looked tired, but he was most concerned about her. He'd already asked her if she was okay several times on the way back, and she'd assured him she was. That didn't stop him from worrying, though. She was everything to him, and they'd just been through hell and back. Having her so close— especially in the packhouse—meant the world to him.

Apparently, he wasn't the only one concerned. "Can I get you anything, dear?" Joan asked as she came to sit next to Robin on the sofa. "Maybe something to eat or drink? We all need to replenish ourselves after a fight like that."

Robin smiled. "I think you're right, but I'll take care of it myself if you just tell me where the kitchen is. I'm afraid I didn't pay much attention on the way in."

"Food's taken care of!" Hunter and Conner had disappeared right after they'd come back, and now Brody knew why. They came down the stairs, each of them holding huge platters. The one Hunter set down on the coffee table was laden with cheese, deli meat, and assorted vegetables. The one Conner put next to it had taco meat, tortillas, and all the toppings.

Lori peered at her son. "Hey, that was supposed to be for tomorrow's dinner. Given the circumstances, I think I'll forgive you. Thank you, honey."

When a stack of plates had been fetched and everyone dug in, Dawn made her way over to Brody and Robin, where they sat on the couch. She had dark circles under her eyes, and she'd probably just finished a shift at the hospital before the events of the evening. Even so, her eyes shone with delight as she held out her hand to Robin. "I haven't been able to officially introduce myself, but I'm Dawn, Brody's sister. I just want to let you know you were great in there tonight."

Robin pressed her fingers to her forehead,

looking embarrassed. "I did my best, but it's all thanks to Brody. If it weren't for him, I wouldn't even know how to walk on all fours, much less fight. Besides, if anyone deserves congratulations, it's you and your mom. I've obviously never seen anything like that before, but it was incredible."

Dawn waved off her praise with a rolled-up piece of ham before she bit into it. "Nah, that's just an old family talent that goes back centuries. You're the star, and I won't let you think otherwise!"

Brody's plate was heavy with food, and his stomach demanded him to get it into his mouth faster, but he was more interested in seeing how his mate and sister were getting along so quickly. Dawn had been excited to meet her, and Brody had a feeling this was going to be the start of a great friendship. He felt more at home than he had in a long time, and it was good. Really good.

Robin had just said something else about Brody's training capabilities when Max spoke up. "You know, if we want to talk about training, I think we really need to commend these two young wolves over here." He gestured at Hunter and Conner, sitting on the floor in front of the coffee table and stuffing their faces without bothering to use plates.

Rex was standing near the fireplace. He hadn't yet helped himself to the meal, following the old pack protocol of ensuring everyone else had nourishment before taking any for himself. He put his hands on his hips and nodded in agreement. "Absolutely. You haven't had much chance to get in on any real battles yet, but you certainly proved yourselves tonight."

A deep sense of satisfaction filled Brody's chest. While they'd been at Edith's mansion, his focus had mostly been on Robin, but that didn't mean he'd missed the work the boys did. "I agree. Young wolves often make the mistake of thinking they need to take the enemy down alone, but it's about teamwork. You fell back and let someone else lead the attack when you were injured. You stepped in to help defend those who needed it, and you managed to keep yourselves from getting hurt. You've been listening, and I'm honored by that."

Rex glanced at Max as he stepped forward. "Speaking of honor, there's something else we need to discuss."

There had been some general chitchat up until this point, but Rex's serious tone brought the room to silence.

"Brody."

He couldn't quite read the look in Rex's eyes, but Brody, too, felt just how heavy this moment was. He set his plate down and stood. If a punishment was coming for turning a human into one of them, he'd gladly take it. Hell, he'd take anything as long as it meant he had Robin by his side, and he was prepared to say that as soon as Rex doled out his penalty.

"A lot has happened over the last few weeks," Rex began, his blue eyes intense. "Brody, you've turned a human into one of us."

Here it came. He was ready for it.

"But you came to us, and you took responsibility for it. When you and Max discovered the body of that young woman, you didn't wait around for the police to find her. You knew it was important to get to the bottom of it, and you volunteered to organize a party to search for clues about what had happened."

Brody felt everyone's eyes on him. This wasn't what he'd expected at all.

"For the last part of what I'd like to discuss, we have to go back further than just the last few weeks. Brody, you've always said you're not into pack politics, but the training you've done with our youth shows you care a hell of a lot about this family and the pack that surrounds it. I've already discussed this with our other ranking members, both past and present, but very little discussion was required. Brody, I'd like you to officially be third in command." Rex reached out his hand.

As Brody looked around at the rest of his family, it all felt completely surreal. Since they were pups, they'd known that Rex would become the Alpha. There'd never been a doubt that Max would be the beta. But him? Brody? He'd never thought he'd be a ranking member, and he didn't think anyone else had, either. To know now that they'd paid far more attention than he'd realized, far more than he thought he deserved, was overwhelming. The backs of his eyes stung as he reached out his hand. "I don't know what to say."

"Say you'll take over some of my duties at the pack meetings," Max joked as he clapped a hand on Brody's shoulder. "You always covered for me when we were kids, so why change anything?"

"I don't know. I think this changes a lot of things." Brody couldn't begin to explain just how different it felt, standing there with his brothers beside him, truly accepted not just as part of the pack but as part of its leadership.

"No, it doesn't," Rex insisted. "This is how it always should've been."

"Oh, Jimmy," Joan said tearfully, patting her husband on the knee. "Just look at our boys."

"Give them a minute, and they'll be wrestling on the floor again, just like they always used to back in the day," Dawn commented with a smile.

"I won every single one of those," Max reminded her.

"Only when I hit my head on the hearth and almost blacked out," Rex pointed out.

Brody nodded. "That's probably true, but don't forget that you two had to gang up to have any chance of beating me."

"All right, all right." Rex pulled Brody in for a one-armed hug and thumped his back. He let go and came over to Robin, leaning down to take her hand. "I think it goes without saying, but welcome to the Glenwood pack. I can already tell you fit in perfectly."

She blushed and smiled. "Thank you."

The teary-eyed moment moved on to more congratulations, bragging, and eating. When Brody made his way back to Robin, she touched his knee and leaned in close where only he could hear.

"There's something I'd like to talk to you about. Privately."

"Then let's go take a walk. There's not going to be anything private here tonight." Brody took her by the hand and led her outside.

Selene shone brightly over them, silvering Robin's hair, reminding Brody of just how gorgeous she looked in her wolf form. "Are you sure you aren't too tired for this? I mean, after tonight."

She slipped her hand into his as they made their way down the path and into the woods, where strips of moonlight skipped across them every few steps. "I'm completely exhausted, but it doesn't matter."

"Well, of course it—"

"No, it doesn't," she insisted. "It doesn't matter because what I have to tell you can't wait any longer. I've wasted enough time already, and I'm not going to waste another second."

Rex's announcement had turned out to be a good one, but Brody knew there was no guarantee that this would turn out the same way. He waited, trying to be patient.

"What we did tonight..." she began. "I don't even know exactly how to describe it. I was fighting for my life, those of the women Dr. Watson and Edith had already killed, and those of you and your family. I did things I never would've thought I'd be able to do, things that were visceral, powerful. It makes me feel like a completely different person."

"Is that bad?" he dared to ask.

"No." Her answer was followed by a gentle laugh like starlight. "I wondered at first. I didn't know how to be a wolf. There's still a lot more I have yet to learn, but I like knowing that I have the pack behind me, ready to stand with me. I've always been close to my family, but this is different. I also like knowing that I've got you by my side."

They stepped into a small clearing, and Brody pulled her close. He felt the pressure of her body against his, and his wolf let him know that it still went just as crazy around her as it always had. "You don't know how much I like hearing you say that."

"I was hoping you would." Her breath was soft against his lips as she spoke. "Brody, I just wanted you to know that I've come to accept what I am. I've also realized that what comes along with being your mate isn't as scary as I thought. I was so worried that I was getting trapped again. I can see now that this isn't about being controlled by you or being subservient to you. It's about being your partner, about the two of us going through everything together. I've never felt this way about anyone before."

"Me, neither." Brody pressed his forehead to hers. "So you're saying you'll accept me as your mate?"

"I wouldn't want anyone else," she whispered.

Brody kissed her lips, feeling the warm velvet against his own. His wolf had calmed, no longer raging within him, but satisfied to know that Robin was right there with him and always would be.

Slowly, regretfully, he pulled away. This was all so incredible, but he couldn't leave it at that. Not when he knew what he knew. "Robin, you absolutely took my breath away tonight. You fought so passionately, and you were so brave. You had every reason to leave that place and let us take care of the rest of it, but you refused."

She put her hands against his chest and looked away as she smiled. "You're going to have to stop praising me, or it'll start going to my head."

"You deserve that praise, but I want to tell you the other thing I noticed tonight."

His tone made her look back up at him. "What is it?"

"I've told you I can hear your thoughts when we're in our wolf forms," he started.

"Right. I'm sure they were a hot, jumbled mess tonight."

"Not as much as you'd think." She'd been focused on her fighting, as had he. "The thing is, there are other matters I can sense about you when we've shifted. Like the baby."

"What?"

"You're pregnant, Robin."

She pulled back from him just enough so she could touch her stomach. "Are you sure? How could you know before I do?"

He rolled a shoulder. "Like I said, it's a shifter thing. Maybe it's a change in your hormones or something, but I'm not going to pretend I know the science behind it. It's not like I could sense it the moment we conceived, but I can now. If you had more experience in your wolf, you would notice it, too."

"Oh my god." She lifted her hand to her mouth, and her eyes widened. "Brody, we're going to have a baby?" A single tear streamed down her cheek.

He caught it with his thumb and rubbed it away. "Are you upset?"

"No. I'm so happy!" The tears came harder now, and he pulled her into his chest. "I've wanted a child for so long, but I thought I'd missed the chance."

Brody felt tears behind his eyes as he smoothed her hair and kissed her head. "Me, too. I can't wait to do this together."

He kissed her again when she lifted her head and felt the tender urgency in her lips as they grazed against his. Brody tangled her hair in his fingers, cradling her head and bringing her closer. She was what he'd been looking for his whole life, and he'd been a fool to think he could settle for anything less than this sort of perfection.

Her breasts pressed against him, reminding him of just how marvelous their previous rendezvous had been. Her tongue slipped past his lips, seeking more than a celebratory kiss. She roved along his tongue, pulling it into her mouth and possessing him. Robin stretched against him, her hands roaming, her body wanting. "Mark me."

The words made his fangs emerge in an instant. There in the woods, by the light of Selene, Brody swept her hair to the side and delicately sank his teeth into the warm flesh between her neck and shoulder. Robin inhaled sharply but then melted against him as he gently licked the tender wound and trailed kisses along her neck. He took her by the waist and brought her down to the bed of pine needles beneath them. Brody didn't care about the chill of the ground, only the warmth of her body against his as cotton and denim slipped away. They didn't have the desperation they did last time, the primitive need to strip their clothes away as quickly as they could before anything had the chance to stop them. This time, it was slow and deliberate, something they had all the time in the world for.

Nothing was going to stop them or make them change their minds. This was it, and along with their clothes, they set aside all the fears and doubts they'd had to navigate to get to this point. None of that mattered when her fingers traced his collarbone and her kisses outlined his shoulders. There was nothing for him to think about other than the way her bare skin felt against his as he pulled her close for another long, sensual kiss.

When Brody had pulled away the last bit of clothing that hid her from him, he marveled at the beauty of her body as she settled astride him. Her face, so sweet, yet full of desire as she found his erection. Her full breasts, soft and tempting, moving with her sudden intake of breath as he slipped his fingers between her thighs and touched her delicate folds, already slick for him. His free hand glided over the slight tuck of her waist just before it flared out to those luscious hips. His fingers and eyes lingered over the curve of her stomach, that sacred place where even now, she was caring for the new life they'd' be bringing into the world. That knowledge, combined with the love in her eyes, made him want to bask in this moment forever, to know that he'd finally found his soulmate. It was in their bodies and their souls, and the swelling of emotion within him added to the riotous pleasure of his body. She was right there with him, stroking him, loving him, yet he still wanted more.

She knew just how to touch him, making it hard to concentrate as he buried his fingers into the sultry sweetness of her, rubbing his thumb in slow circles over her until he could see the agony of his efforts on her face.

Her strokes moved faster, the skin of her fingers soft but the strength demanding, and the nails of her free hand dug into his shoulder as she fought against the coming spasms to keep herself upright. Her breath came in desperate pants and then little cries of pleasure as he brought her to her peak. Her hips jerked and her core clenched, possessed by his love for her as it moved through her body. Brody watched her and knew he'd never seen anything so beautiful. He wanted to see it again. She could make him lose control, and he wanted to see that he could do the same to her. When her shoulders sagged and he knew it had passed, he moved his fingers against her again, tantalizing and teasing. Robin clutched at his wrist, but she didn't pull him away. Her head rolled on her shoulders as she rode his hand. Those same seizures of indulgence overtook her once again, making her jerk and gasp until she couldn't take any more.

Brody took her hips and guided her down on top of him, feeling the slow, tight sinking of himself within her. His eyes rolled to the moonlit sky above them as he reveled in the delight of her body. She was still sighing with the aftereffects of her first two climaxes as he pulled her down, bringing her breast to his mouth. He flicked his tongue over the silken skin of her nipple until it hardened. Brody lost himself in the delight of her body as she rocked her hips, lifting just enough before she came back down around him once again.

Taking her other nipple and drawing it into his mouth, he felt the rumble of pleasure in his chest as he curved his hands and locked them around her luxurious backside. He grasped her as she rocked, their bodies locked in a primal choreography that brought her surging upward once again. Brody could feel it within her this time, the clasping and clutching and needing, and he gladly tumbled right along with her.

He held her against his chest, their arms and legs entwined, with only the light of the moon to see them. Robin was his everything, and he thanked Selene for bringing her to him.

20

EPILOGUE: 6 MONTHS LATER

"OPEN BIG AND WIDE FOR ME, NOVA. OH, MY goodness! You're very good at that!" Robin leaned over to examine the little girl's mouth. When her patient tried to say something, Robin pulled her hands back. "What was that?"

"What are you looking for in there?" She squirmed in the exam chair, her eyes big.

"I'm just making sure all your teeth are healthy," Robin explained. "You know how you go to the doctor sometimes?"

Nova nodded. "They always tell me I'm getting bigger and stronger, and they give me a sticker when we're done."

Robin couldn't help but smile. This little girl was

just adorable. Of course, she thought that about most of her patients these days now that she was working for a small pediatric office. "Coming to the dentist is just like that, but for your teeth. We have to make sure they stay clean and healthy. I also happen to have a very cool box of stickers you can look through when you're done."

"Really?" Needing no further convincing, Nova opened her mouth wide once again.

Robin hummed to herself as she worked. She wished that she'd changed jobs a long time ago instead of sticking things out with the horrid Dr. Watson, but she tried not to think about that too much. The most important thing was that she was finally doing what she really loved. She was happy, and so were her patients.

"All done!" she said a short time later. "You've been doing a great job keeping your teeth clean, so keep it up!"

"Okay!" Nova hopped down from the chair as Robin stood, and her eyes immediately locked on Robin's belly. "Are you having a baby?"

"That's a rude thing to ask, Nova," her mother chided.

"It's all right," Robin assured her. "I am, and I'm very excited about it."

"Is it going to be a girl or a boy?" Nova chewed her lip.

"We don't know just yet. We decided we're going to wait and find out when it's born." She and Brody had been waiting for this moment in their lives for so long, and it didn't matter what they had. Her days were filled with jolts of joy every time she accidentally rubbed against her belly or felt the wriggling of life within her, little reminders of just what was coming.

"Good for you," Nova's mother said as she picked up her purse and slung the strap over her shoulder. "We decided not to find out the gender of our youngest. Everyone in the family completely freaked out, like it was the strangest thing in the world. I hope you don't have to deal with that."

Unclipping the bib from around Nova's neck, Robin smiled and shook her head. The Glenwoods had been thrilled about the news, and they hadn't questioned either her or Brody once on their choices. Her own family had been equally excited. They'd welcomed Brody as part of their family, and Robin's mother was constantly trying to take Robin out shopping for baby clothes. "No. Not at all. Now let's go get you that sticker, Nova."

When Robin had brought them to the front desk

and Nova was eagerly digging through a big box of stickers to see which one she wanted to bring home, Dr. Sweeney stepped out from seeing her last patient. "Oh, Robin. I wanted to talk to you about something, if you have a moment."

Robin smiled at her new boss. "Sure."

"We're trying to get the vacation calendar filled out for next year. I know things are never certain with babies, but if you could pop into the system and fill out your estimated maternity leave, that would be really helpful. Don't worry, though. I'm not going to hold you to it if your little one decides to come early or late." Dr. Sweeney beamed softly as she looked down at Robin's bump.

"Sure, I can do that." She couldn't imagine what it would've been like to try to take maternity leave while still working for Dr. Watson. Everything at her new office felt so easy.

"Great, thank you. Oh, and you remember Daniel Fletcher that you saw a few days ago?"

"Of course." The boy had been absolutely terrified when he'd come in for his cleaning. His mother had mentioned that he was on the autism spectrum and had sensory issues, and it was obvious that she was worried about how it was going to go.

"His mother called me yesterday," Dr. Sweeney

continued. "She wanted to make sure she talked to me personally to let me know what an excellent job you did with Daniel. She said she'd never taken him to any kind of dental appointment and had such a good experience."

"That's wonderful to hear."

"You're telling me!" her boss said with a laugh. "It's not always easy to find good people, but I obviously did."

As Robin finished up for the day and disinfected her exam room, she sighed with satisfaction. It was true that the paychecks there were smaller, but the work was so much more satisfying, and now that Brody had moved into her bungalow, she didn't have to carry the burden of everything on her own anymore.

A short time later, she heard a deep rumble behind her as she pulled into the garage. Brody parked his bike next to her car and kissed her before she could even get out of the vehicle. "You seem to be in a good mood today," she noted.

"How could I not be when I get to come home to you? Both of you, actually." He stroked his hand gently across her belly.

Robin leaned into him for another kiss. Her wolf was content inside of her. In a way, she had to wonder if the pregnancy would've felt this fabulous, or if it'd worked to her advantage that she hadn't been blessed with a baby until now. Yes, she realized as soon as the thought formed, because she wouldn't have wanted to do this with anyone but Brody. "Even so, you seem happier than usual."

They stepped into the kitchen, where the home-made chicken stew Brody had put together before he left was simmering in the slow cooker. He lifted the lid and gave it a stir, sending that delectable scent even thicker through the air. "I had a good meeting with Rex and Max this morning, discussing the future of the pack and what we needed to do to make sure everything stayed on track. I have to admit, I actually like this whole third in command thing more than I thought I would."

Robin smiled to herself. She'd hardly known him for more than a few weeks when he'd gotten that promotion, but even she'd been able to tell it was a badge of honor for him. Ever since, he'd started spending a lot more time at the packhouse, eagerly discussing and suggesting ways they could keep their members safe and happy.

Brody added some extra minced garlic and a sprig of thyme to the stew before replacing the lid. "I also had a great session with the younger wolves today. They're really excelling in their training, and even the young pups are learning how to work together. It's such an amazing thing to see how they change as they grow."

Robin set her purse down and went to the freezer to get a package of dinner rolls, which sounded like the perfect addition to the meal. She turned on the oven to let it warm up. "I imagine you'll get to see the same thing happening with our little one."

"Speaking of our little one, that's probably the other reason I'm so happy. Come here." He took her by the hand and pulled her into the baby's room.

Brody had used the second bedroom as a studio when he'd first moved in. There'd been little debate as to where the two of them would live when they decided to move in together since Robin loved her home so much. His easels and extra supplies had been moved to the tattoo shop, the walls had been emptied, and the dark curtains over the windows had been taken down to make way for the nursery.

"I scheduled a day off work and away from the packhouse tomorrow," he said as he stepped over to several large tote bags that sat on the floor. "This morning, I went down to the hardware store and picked up all of this."

Robin marveled as she saw the tarp, paint rollers, and masking tape. The gallons of paint were marked on the top with the lovely shade of sage green they'd picked out. Another can of pure white would serve as the trim color. A surge of excitement zipped through her. "You're going to paint tomorrow?"

"It's about time since this little one only has a few more months before it's ready to meet the world," Brody reasoned. "Besides, we'll still need to get all the furniture put in and the curtains up. There's a lot to keep me busy when I'm not working."

As he rattled on about all the little details he wanted to work on for the nursery, Robin couldn't believe her luck. Here was a man who cared about her and wanted the best for their little family. He worked hard, and he liked to spend time with his brothers and pack, but Robin and the baby were never far from his mind. He was the very definition of a perfect mate, and she was so glad that they'd found each other.

Brody came around behind her and wrapped his arms around her waist, or at least where her waist used to be. His hands rubbed up and down on each side of her belly, and he rested his chin on her shoulder. "You should probably go put your feet up. You've been working all day."

It sounded wonderful, but what she had right there was too good to miss out on. Robin leaned into him and closed her eyes. "So have you."

"I don't mind. Oh." He stopped moving his hands, and he even held his breath as he waited. "There it is again!"

Robin smiled as the baby kicked. "Little One always seems to hold onto its biggest kicks for when you're around. I think it'll be a fighter like its daddy."

He shook his head and nuzzled his face into the side of her neck, dotting kisses along her skin. "Oh, it's a fighter, all right. But I think it gets that from you."

THE END

If you enjoyed Brody and Robin's story, read on for a preview of Max and Sarah's story, *Wolf's Midlife Secret Child*!

MAX

"Ugh! How can anyone actually wear these?"

Sarah allowed a glimmer of a smile to cross over her face as she looked at her daughter holding out a pair of men's bikini briefs by its string. Ava may not know much of the outside world, but she was still just as much of a sixteen-year-old girl as she'd be in other circumstances. "I've yet to figure that out, honey, and frankly, I don't want to. At least we have the luxury of a washing machine and dryer instead of doing it by hand like people had to back in the day."

Ava glared over her head as someone stomped through the Greystone packhouse on the floor above them. "I don't know. There might've been some benefits to that."

"Yeah? Like what?"

Her daughter rolled her shoulder as she poured detergent into the washing machine, keeping her head back as she chucked the manties into the machine. "Well, maybe not if I had to wash a load of *these*, but I don't know. Doing it outside, I guess?"

Sarah pulled the next shirt from the basket at her feet and laid it carefully over the ironing board. The dryer beeped, letting her know the towels were done. "Are you really going to tell me you'd rather touch all these dirty clothes with your hands while you scrubbed them in filthy water against a washboard?"

Moving aside the next load of dirty laundry, Ava gagged. "Never mind, you're right. I just don't see why the people in this packhouse can't wash their own clothes."

Sarah had no answer for that. Her mouth hardened into a grim line, knowing Ava wouldn't have these kinds of responsibilities if it weren't for her. Sure, she'd be expected to do chores. Sarah knew she'd never let any child of hers just run around with all the freedom in the world and no responsibility. Ava had the opposite, and there was nothing Sarah could do about it.

"Sarah!" The thundering footsteps overhead were now thundering down the basement steps, sending bits of dust shaking down from the old wooden boards and making the mason jars in the storage space rattle.

Her stomach tightened, and she felt her shoulders hunch up around her ears, but Sarah forced them back down again. She wouldn't let Edward know what he made her feel whenever she saw or even heard him. He had enough power, and she wouldn't give him a shred more of it. "Yes?" she asked, pointedly focusing on her ironing as she created a perfect crease down one sleeve.

"Where's my blue shirt? The button-down one? You said you'd have it clean before tonight." Coming around from the stairwell and into the laundry area of the basement, Edward Greystone glowered at his daughter as he put his fists on either side of the belly that lapped his belt.

"It's right here, as promised." Sarah set down the iron and lifted the blue shirt in question from the nearby rack. "I even got all those grease stains off the front. You should be more careful the next time you decide to gorge yourself on bratwurst."

He snatched it from her grasp. "Don't try to

lecture me. You just turned forty. You ought to know your place in this pack by now."

Giving him a mock smile and wide eyes, Sarah tented the fingers of one hand over her collarbone. "Oh, you remembered! I thought you'd forgotten today was my birthday. Is that why you wanted your best shirt? So we could all go out to dinner and celebrate? I'll be sure to put on my best rags."

His fist tightened around the shoulder of the shirt he held in his hand, pressing wrinkles into the freshly ironed fabric. "You're lucky I even let you live after the disgrace you brought to this pack, Sarah."

"I'm not sure I'd call this living, *Dad*." Sarah flipped her hand around her to indicate the dusty basement, including the shabby bathroom with a leaky faucet and the makeshift bedroom she and Ava shared in the back corner.

"I am your Alpha!" Edward roared, taking a step forward. Spittle flew from his mouth and smacked onto the unfinished concrete floor. "You and your brat have been an embarrassment to this pack for years. Learn to obey me, or else." He gritted his teeth, shaking one angry hand toward Ava.

Sarah's heart clenched, but it was a different type of fear that shook her this time. She straightened her shoulders and lifted her chin as she stepped slightly to the side, putting herself between her father and daughter. There was little she could do if he decided to lose his temper, especially with this damn silver collar lying so heavily around her neck, but that wouldn't stop her from trying. She'd already done wrong by Ava in so many ways, but she couldn't let things go any further. "I'm sorry, Father." Her eyes held his steadily.

"As you should be." Still clutching his precious damn shirt, he turned and stormed back up the stairs. "Janice, where the hell is my cell phone? I can't find it anywhere."

When the door slammed behind him, a tiny giggle had Sarah turning toward her daughter in shock. "What's so funny?"

Ava's eyes were wide and glistening, and her lips were pressed together as she tried to hold back her laughter. She glanced at the ceiling and shrugged innocently.

Sarah would've thought Ava would be terrified after that encounter with her so-called grandfather, but that didn't seem to be the case. "Do you know where his phone is?"

Casually opening the dryer and pulling out a

clean towel, Ava began folding it on top of the washing machine. "How should I know where his phone is? It's not my responsibility to keep track of it. He might be surprised to find it under the bathroom sink, though. He really ought to be more careful."

Despite the desperation surrounding their situation, Sarah burst out laughing as she turned back to her ironing. "You little sneak! I have to admire your efforts, though. I'm just concerned that you'll get into more trouble than we can handle if you get caught."

Ava lifted her chin in a way that reminded Sarah too much of herself. "I'm not going to get caught."

"You don't know that," Sarah said quietly, wishing there was some way she could've protected Ava from this life.

More movement could be heard over their heads, something they were used to at this point. Sarah and Ava were only allowed in the rest of the packhouse when tasked with chores, returning to the basement as soon as they'd finished. They'd learned to recognize footsteps and determine where they were going. It definitely wasn't Edward this time; the steps were too light. Sarah's shoulders relaxed slightly.

Ava set another towel on the stack and reached back into the dryer. She stuck her nail under the silver collar around her neck and itched for a moment. "I'm careful, Mom. More careful than you can even imagine."

Sarah's heart twisted as her eyes rested on that horrid band of metal. She'd cried openly when a tiny collar had been clamped around Ava's neck when she was just a toddler, a punishment Sarah had thought her daughter wouldn't have to suffer along with her. They'd changed it out as she'd grown, but it never made Sarah feel any better about it. They both knew what it meant.

The collar was just the minimum punishment that could be inflicted on them if they didn't behave. Sarah could throw caution to the wind for her own sake, but not for her daughter's. "If you're up there causing trouble, then it's too much of a risk, Ava. I can't have anything happen to you."

Ava's eyes sparked once again. "I'll be fine, Mom. See, I—" She stopped, and her eyes flicked over to the stairs.

Sarah had been focusing on her too much to notice the quiet thump of the basement door. She turned to see her mother, carefully setting her feet down in just the right places to make as few creaks and squeaks as possible as she descended the staircase.

Janice glanced back up at the door when she reached the bottom of the steps, then hurried over to Sarah, holding out a single cupcake on a small plate. "Happy birthday, dear."

"Oh, Mom." Sarah took it in her hands as though it were made of gold. They weren't allowed niceties like this. A sugary treat might be an everyday occurrence for others, but not for her. She knew just how big of a risk her mother had taken by doing such a thing. "You didn't have to."

"Yes, I did." Janice looked like she was going to cry as she pulled a lighter and candle out of her pocket, even though she was trying her best to be brave. "Everyone deserves to have their birthday celebrated."

Holding the cupcake as her mother put the candle down through the frosting, Sarah felt tears burn the backs of her eyes. She'd tried not to think about it, but it was impossible. This was her son's birthday as well. How could she ever forget the day he came into the world and made her a mother for the first time? He'd changed her entire life, but Sarah knew she'd probably never get the chance to tell him so. At forty, she always thought she'd be driving her kids to soccer practice and looking at colleges with them. Instead, there she was, demoted to the lowest member of her pack, living a life of servitude with her daughter. "I've been trying not to think about it."

"I know, dear." Janice reached out to touch Sarah's hair, her sad eyes whisking over her face. She must not have liked what she saw because she soon returned her attention to the cupcake. "What are you going to wish for this year?"

Sarah closed her eyes. She remembered a time when she still believed in birthday wishes, when she'd sat at the dining table upstairs with the rest of the pack around her, trying to decide to wish for a pony or a kitten. There were times as a child when she'd resented the way the adults ran her life, when they wouldn't let her go where she wanted in the woods, or when she couldn't spend the night at a friend's house or participate in a pack run because she hadn't brought up her grades. Life had seemed so unfair, and she'd been bitter about the way she'd been imprisoned by rules and regulations.

Independence had come to mean something so much more than that.

Sarah didn't want a pony or a kitten. She

wouldn't wish for a new designer dress or a gorgeous car. There was only one thing she wanted as she opened her eyes and focused on the flame. Freedom.

With a long, slow breath, she blew out the candle.

———

ALSO BY MEG RIPLEY

ALL AVAILABLE ON AMAZON

Shifter Nation Universe

Marked Over Forty Series

Fated Over Forty Series

Wild Frontier Shifters Series

Special Ops Shifters: L.A. Force Series

Special Ops Shifters: Dallas Force Series

Special Ops Shifters Series (original D.C. Force)

Werebears of Acadia Series

Werebears of the Everglades Series

Werebears of Glacier Bay Series

Werebears of Big Bend Series

Dragons of Charok Universe

Daddy Dragon Guardians Series

Shifters Between Worlds Series

Dragon Mates: The Complete Dragons of Charok
Universe Collection (Includes Daddy Dragon Guardians
and Shifters Between Worlds)

More Shifter Romance Series

Beverly Hills Dragons Series

Dragons of Sin City Series

Dragons of the Darkblood Secret Society Series

Packs of the Pacific Northwest Series

Compilations

Forever Fated Mates Collection

Shifter Daddies Collection

Early Novellas

Mated By The Dragon Boss

Claimed By The Werebears of Green Tree

Bearer of Secrets

Rogue Wolf

ABOUT THE AUTHOR

Steamy shifter romance author Meg Ripley is a Seattle native who's relocated to New England. She can often be found whipping up her next tale curled up in a local coffee house with a cappuccino and her laptop.

Download *Alpha's Midlife Baby,* the steamy prequel to Meg's Fated Over Forty series, when you sign up for the Meg Ripley Insiders newsletter!

Sign up by visiting www.authormegripley.com

Connect with Meg

amazon.com/Meg-Ripley/e/B00Z8I9AXW
tiktok.com/@authormegripley
facebook.com/authormegripley
instagram.com/megripleybooks
bookbub.com/authors/meg-ripley
goodreads.com/megripley
pinterest.com/authormegripley

Printed in Great Britain
by Amazon

43430230R00148